PASSION AND SURRENDER

"Come along, darling. We must get on...."

Katherine pulled herself together and smiled at him. She was his wife. Once again she reminded herself that this was his day, and she was so very lucky and happy, too.

She sat down in the car, smiling, shaking a little with emotion, her hand tight-clasped in her husband's.

Little Nicholas Haddon skipped up to the car and flung his precious confetti over Katherine, screaming:

"Aunty Katrine, Aunty Katrine!"

Katherine brushed away the confetti and waved at the child. The car moved on. Once out of sight of the crowd, Robert took his beautiful bride in his arms. Now there was no room in her heart for anything but him, as she surrendered to his kiss.

Second Marriage

Denise Robins

AVON
PUBLISHERS OF BARD, CAMELOT AND DISCUS BOOKS

AVON BOOKS
A division of
The Hearst Corporation
959 Eighth Avenue
New York, New York 10019
Copyright © 1952 by Denise Robins
Published by arrangement with Hodder & Stoughton Ltd.
Library of Congress Catalog Card Number: 79-64704
ISBN: 0-380-45492-0

First Avon Printing, August, 1979

Second Marriage

1

THE guard was holding up his flag and had the whistle to his lips as Judy rushed down the platform. The boy who was leaning anxiously out of the window of a third-class carriage opened the door and pulled her in.

"Good old Ju! Late as usual!"

He grinned at her affectionately as she flung herself, giggling, into the corner opposite him.

"Oh! What a flap I've been in! The worst traffic jam you could imagine—my bus was paralysed. But I've made it."

"You generally do, but one of these days you'll get left behind, my poppet!" he laughed.

The train moved slowly out of Victoria Station. Boy and girl smiled at each other. Easy to see they were brother and sister. The same short, rather stocky build, and thick curly blue-grey eyes with long dark lashes. But whereas Judy had hair the colour of burnished copper. The same handsome a curving, wilful mouth, with full sweet lips and square, determined little chin, her brother, Pat, had more sensitive, fine-cut lips and less determination in his face. Judy obviously had the stronger disposition of the two. She was also the older by a year and a bit. Pat had only recently celebrated his eighteenth birthday and been called up for his Military Service. This was his first leave. Judy had telephoned to Colchester, where he was stationed, to suggest that they should meet on this train so that they could have a talk alone before reaching home.

"I am a bit worried about Mummy," she had said mysteriously. "Ever since you've been gone I've noticed a change in her, and I don't think it's only due to your absence—even though she does dote on you."

7

And the last few words had been said without rancour, because Judy's devotion to young Pat almost equalled her mother's. He was a darling; a little shy and still at the *gauche* age, but with a stronge sense of humour and a passion for music. Dance music! If they hadn't loved him so much, Judy and her mother had often laughingly said, they would disown him because of that constant wail of "swing" which used to issue from his bedroom. And he had even threatened to learn the clarinet!

But now he was in the Army for two years.

"Before we begin to talk, tell me how you like being a soldier," Judy asked him, still out of breath and puffing a little. The June day had been hot in town. Her cheeks were flushed and she had pulled off her hat and started to comb back her curls. She looked exceedingly pretty, and Pat Green had quite decided that he would never take on a girl friend unless he could find one as good-looking—not that he ever told Ju what he really thought. He more often addressed her as "Ugly Mug" or "Snub Nose."

He spoke briefly about his life in barracks. He "quite liked" it, but it was pretty uncomfortable and the food "*grim*" after Mum's good cooking. Some of the other chaps were pretty rough—but he'd found another swing-lover and they were going to get together and form a dance band as soon as possible, which would make life more bearable for Pat.

"You don't think you'll be sent to Korea to fight Chinese Communists, do you?" Judy asked anxiously.

He grinned at her.

"Not yet."

"Mum would die of horror!" said Judy.

"I bet she wouldn't. She'd say it was my job. She's always jolly decent the way she avoids fussing a chap."

Judy's smile suddenly faded as she thought about their mother.

"Yes, I know she doesn't often show her feelings if she thinks we want something—even when *she* doesn't want it. She's terribly good."

Pat handed a packet of cigarettes to his sister, who shook her head, then he lit one for himself.

"Well, we're lucky enough to have a carriage to ourselves,

so we can talk. What *is* wrong with Mum? Why all the mystery?"

"That's what *I* don't know."

"She's not ill, is she?" Pat's brows knit and he was immediately full of forebodings.

"No. At least I don't think so. But she's frightfully restless and peculiar. Keeps asking if I think you really like the cottage—of course it's so small—or if I need more clothes and a better time. And then she's always going out for walks—and not just to exercise the dogs. And I've seen her look quite odd while she's been reading or writing a letter. I'm sure somethings on her mind, anyhow."

Pat looked at his sister thoughtfully through his long lashes.

"I expect it's money troubles. It generally is. She's had a packetful, bringing us up since Dad died."

"Well, I don't know that it *is* money."

"Or is it because she's rather a lot alone—with me away and you at the shop all day?"

"But she has her friends," said Judy. Then added with a grimace: "You know what a lot she thinks of Robert Tracy's opinion. Whenever anything goes wrong with the roof or the chickens or anything else she gets him round. He's Adviser-in-Chief."

"He's quite a knowledgeable chap."

"Well, I can't stand him," said Judy.

"He's been a jolly good friend to us."

Judy hunched her shoulders. She was less tolerant than her brother and a little more jealous in temperament.

Ever since their beloved father had died, while they were still small school-children, their mother had been everything to them and, as young Pat stoutly maintained, done a man's job as well as a woman's. They both remembered Dr. Green. He had had a country practice and been a genial, attractive man who unfortunately contracted a "heart" and died in his middle thirties, before he had time to establish himself. Naturally, as small children, Judy and Pat had had only a small comprehension of all that their mother had suffered— losing an adored husband at such an early age and having them to educate and a home to maintain on the most slender means. David Green had left her the cottage in Cooltye, close to the Sussex Downs, but very little capital, which had dwindled with taxation, and supplied a meagre income which Katherine Green had had to augment with her pen. She wrote charming stories for children, and sold them. The young Greens owed their good education to those stories. They were not spoiled or ungrateful. They had the greater respect for the hard way Mummy worked, both in the cottage and the garden—and on her typewriter. There seemed little that Mum could not do. But their love had something of a possessive quality, and Judy personally had always resented the fact that their near neighbour, Robert Tracy, was Mummy's great friend and confidant, and came so often to their home.

He was a popular man in the district and owned one of the best farms in Sussex. It wasn't that they either of them *disliked* him, but Judy, in particular, had got up against him because of an unfortunate incident (remote now, yet unforgotten) when in her teens she had lost her temper and been rude and difficult in front of "Uncle Robert." For the first and only time he had interfered. He had said:

"You have the finest and most courageous of women for a mother, young Judy. Don't ever say anything hurtful, because I know you'd regret it bitterly later on."

In her heart of hearts she had agreed with him. But she had strongly resented the fact that he had made her feel so ashamed. She had never really forgiven him, in spite of his efforts to make amends—for it was he who had given her Titus, the Staffordshire bull terrier who had become her great pet. Uncle Robert had supper at the cottage every Sunday night. It was a sort of institution. Pat enjoyed talking to him. Robert was an intelligent and broadminded man—now in his early forties and still a bachelor. He had been in the Navy during the war and had given Pat a lot of sound advice which the boy had found helpful. But Judy remained slightly—very slightly—hostile. She thought that Mummy paid too much attention to the things that Uncle Robert said, and she couldn't bear it if Pat was going to follow suit. Of course, it was all childish jealousy, and at heart Judy knew it.

She said now, as the train took them down to Hassocks, which was their station:

"Thinking things over I wouldn't suppose that Mummy was lonely, what with Uncle Robert on the tap and Mrs. Haddon."

They liked Joyce Haddon. She was another "local"—wife of the present doctor who had taken over Daddy's practice.

"Oh, well . . . I must try and find out what's worrying 'me Mum'," said Pat.

"Yes, you make yourself awfully nice and follow her round a bit and see if she'll talk to you," suggested Judy.

Then she started talking about her own affairs.

Six months ago she had started to do "her bit" towards increasing the family exchequer by taking a job as assistant in a combined antique shop and tea rooms in Cooltye. This was at the Dower House—one of the supposed dwellings of Anne Boleyn, and the oldest and most beautiful place in Cooltye, in the main street. Judy earned four pounds a week there and quite enjoyed working amongst lovely furniture and glass and china.

Up in town today she had been lunching with an old school friend, Elizabeth Chapman, who was a few years older than Judy, and with a little more money behind her. She had been trained by Constance Spry and last year opened a florist's shop, which she called *Fleurette*, in the Old Brompton Road. It had been extraordinarily successful, and Elizabeth was anxious for Judy to "go in with her."

"Tony always says you look like a flower yourself, and I think you'd be a great asset as my assistant. All the men would come and buy buttonholes from you!" Elizabeth had laughingly said.

Now Judy adored flowers, and at school she had adored Elizabeth—who looked glamorous and was clever too. And some of the adoration had in recent years been shyly extended to the said Tony, Elizabeth's brother. He was a medical student in his fifth year at Bart's. Even now, as she sat in the train with her brother, Judy felt a little thrill at the remembrance of Tony. He was so very good-looking and clever, like his sister. He had a dark, earnest kind of good looks, and a serious mind as well as a sense of humour which appealed to Judy. Everybody in his family said that Tony was going to make a brilliant doctor one day. Judy liked it because he was so keen on his job. Still, he had a little time to spare for her now and again, and had spent a weekend or two at the cottage, using Pat's room after Pat went away. Tony, of course, wanted her to go up to town and take that job with Elizabeth.

But with all its promised excitement it had not appealed to Judy as much as living at home and going on with her own job. She had always been a "home bird." She couldn't bear the idea of going into lonely "digs" and living away from Mummy. And she was just beginning to pull her weight at the Dower House. No, she wouldn't exchange home life or the antique shop for London and *Fleurette*. As for Tony— the strongest attraction of all—he could always come down to Cooltye when he had a night to spare, or she could nip up to London.

Pat started to tease her.

"Flicking the eyelash a bit at old Tony, aren't you, Sis?"

"Mind your own business," said Judy, red in the face, "and don't call me 'Sis'."

"Well, I hope you're not going to quit the old homestead and leave Mum alone, anyhow," added Pat.

Judy then proceeded to tell her brother exactly what aversion she felt to the mere thought of leaving home or Mummy.

They reached Hassocks. From there the bus dropped them at the top of Tye Hill and they walked, arms linked, down the road to the green hollow in which nestled the little Elizabethan cottage which was their home.

Through a haze of sunshine Tye Cottage looked adorable, its white-washed walls half hidden by honeysuckle and climbing roses, and the wisteria which drooped a delicate green tracery of leaves over the doorway and across the tiny casement windows. It was, as the children always said, like a cottage on a calendar. Hollyhocks in the front garden, roses, roses everywhere. Gay larkspurs and blue delphiniums and one precious oak tree, very large and gnarled, standing just to the right, casting its green shade. From the lowest branch there dangled a swing—reminiscent of childhood. At the back were vegetables and the chickens. And a little way up the road lay Cooltye Village—picturesque and almost unspoilt. In the background the lovely green curves of the Sussex Downs against the pale blue sky.

Cooltye—the home in which Pat and Judy had been brought up. Sleepy, enchanting little Cooltye, with one general shop which was a post office. One garage with its disfiguring petrol pumps. A baker's shop and a butcher's, and a small haberdashery store adjoining the Dower House in which Judy worked, and which was patronized by Americans and foreigners who turned their cars off the main Brighton Road and came through here in order to visit Anne Boleyn's historic home.

Brother and sister now saw the slim figure of a woman (she might have been a girl) in a faded pink cotton frock and with her head tied up in a scarf. She was standing with her back to them, snipping off dead roses. Two golden-brown Corgis lay side by side with their heads on their paws, watching her.

The dogs were the first to see the boy and girl, and darted up to the gate, barking shrilly. The woman in the pink dress swung round. She dropped basket and secateurs and hurried towards her children. She looked younger than ever with that flush of excitement, and the brightness of welcome in her eyes.

"Pat! Judy!"

They rushed to her, and she to them. The next moment they were all embracing, and the dogs rushed around, capering madly, and nobody could hear themselves speak.

Pat drew back from his mother and ran his fingers through his rough curly hair.

"Oh, *gosh*, it's good to be home!" he sighed.

"And so say all of us," seconded Judy. "I thought London was loathsome after Cooltye. And how's 'me Mum'?"

"I'm fine," said Mrs. Green and, with Judy on one side and Pat on the other, walked up the flagged path into her cottage.

Her children were home. That was very good. She was never really happy until she had them back under her wing. Always absurdly anxious that something might have hap-

13

pened to one or the other of them. When Judy went up to town for a day ... she might get run over or be kidnapped. As for Pat, in the Army ... incredible thought, for he was still only a schoolboy to her ... he would obviously be starved or worked to death! Oh, it was *wonderful* to get them home.

"I'll put the kettle on. You'll both be hungry. Then you must tell me everything!" she said.

In the cool, oak-beamed sitting-room, full of old treasures and faded chintzes and rugs, Judy flung herself into a chair, fanning her hot face. But Pat followed his mother into the kitchen to see if he could lend a hand.

"Gosh!" he exclaimed once more. "This is *something*. Mum, you're a pal, you've made my special dripping cake. *And* I see scones. *And* cherry jam. How superb of you!"

Katherine Green switched on the electric kettle. Smiling, she took off her head-scarf. She was fairer than either of her children, with a touch of grey which made her look ash-blonde. Judy had her heart-shaped face. Pat her wide-set, beautiful eyes with the long lashes. But she was thinner than either of her children—too thin—and there were the little lines that life's experience, and some suffering, had etched under her eyes and on either side of the fine-cut lips. She had a charming smile and, when she was happy, looked ten years younger than her age. Pat thought her the most wonderful person in the world. Mother and son understood each other very well, and there was never a day that Katherine Green did not thank God for having such a son as this one. Judy was a darling, but a little less easy to understand, and much more independent. Sometimes Katherine Green was a little frightened of Judy, who could be alarmingly critical and discerning, and was much more typical of direct modern youth than dear old Pat. But they had both been everything to her since she lost David, she reflected now, as she regarded her soldier son. They had occupied all her thoughts and been the sole focus of her interest and ambition, *until* ...

Katherine hardly dared allow herself to go further in her mind than that word "*until*," but a guilty look came into her eyes and she bent over the teapot to hide it. She had a secret ... a very important one ... to tell these two loved children of hers today. And she really did not know how she was ever going to start on it.

But as she made the tea and switched off the kettle she allowed her gaze to wander through the open window, across the garden and the hedgerow to a green field; then over that field to a grey spiral of smoke which drifted from the tall chimney of Robert Tracy's home—Cooltye Farm.

2

TEA was over. Judy and Pat had eaten most of the scones and half the cake. Pat sat back in his armchair, smoking. Katherine Green glanced at him tenderly, smiling now and then as though still trying to convince herself that her "little boy" was really this grown-up man with a hint of down on his upper lip, smoking a cigarette. A man being trained for tank warfare (heaven forbid there should be another world war, she thought fearfully, to sweep her son, amongst so many others, out of this green, grand world).

Unknown to her, Pat was watching his mother. Noting her nervous movements; the way she repeatedly bit her lips or cleared her throat or spoke to Judy with a note of gaiety in her voice which did not ring true. Old Ju was right, he reflected anxiously. Mum was *not* herself. She did not actually look ill. But ill at ease with them, which was so unlike their friendly, easy-going young mother.

It must be a money crisis, he decided. He would find out and if need be send her some of his meagre pay. He could cut down cigarettes and stop the odd beer. Mum came first and if she was hard up . . . yet why should that contingency suddenly arise? She mentioned only the other day that her dividends from her father had not decreased much, and that she had just sold a new book for children, which ought to do well. The sort of exciting adventure stuff he and Ju used to adore, coming from Mummy's pen, when they were small.

What was the trouble? For trouble there was. The longer he watched her, the more Pat agreed with his sister. Mum was *distraite* and almost jittery, getting up and down, emptying ash-trays, unnecessarily, asking Judy the same questions twice over.

16

Then suddenly the unexpected bomb was dropped in the quiet little room. Just as Pat had risen to his feet and announced that he was going down to the garage for a chat with old Ernest on the subject of old motor-bikes.

Katherine Green also rose and, nervously clasping her hands, said:

"Oh, just a moment, Pat darling. I . . . I have something I . . . I want to say to you and Judy."

The two of them looked at their mother enquiringly. Judy was still seated, arms lazily behind her curly head, one of the dogs cuddled on her knee.

Mrs. Green looked back at them almost despairingly. They could not help her. She must help herself. But she had not dreamed it was going to be so difficult—so embarrassing. Then it broke from her:

"Darlings," she said, "wish me luck . . . *please*. I'm so happy. I only want your approval and good wishes to make it all perfect for me. I . . . I'm going to get married again . . . some time at the end of the summer. Perhaps before."

It was out. The incredible news, shattering the peace in the low-ceilinged room with the dark beams and white walls and the sun filtering through the open casements. Judy's arms dropped to her sides. A look of incredulity, almost horror, came into her eyes. Pat stood rigid. He went a little pale, then red. Judy was the first to speak, her voice raised.

"You are *what* . . . Mummy? Going to be *married*, did you say? But it can't be true."

"Good lord," muttered Pat, and swallowed hard.

Mrs. Green looked at them with that guilty yet pleading expression in her beautiful eyes. Her cheeks flamed. She said:

"Why not? Why shouldn't I marry again? I'm not an old crone yet . . ." she laughed nervously; "only in my early forties. Lots of women marry for the first time at forty. Look at Miss Baker, here in Cooltye . . . marrying that Canadian during the war."

"But that was different!" exclaimed Judy.

"Why different, darling? Isn't a widow entitled to marry again? After all . . . I've been a widow for a long time. It's been rather lonely . . . without your father . . ." Her voice broke. "You know how I loved him, don't you? How I've missed him. I devoted my life to you children. But now . . ."

"Now what?" Judy was the spokesman. Pat seemed tongue-tied, dumbfounded by his mother's announcement. But the girl was flushed and furious. Obviously not taking it well. Katherine's heart sank. She had anticipated some slight reluctance on her daughter's part to accept the news. But not an out-and-out dislike of the whole idea. She made another desperate attempt to capture the sympathy and understanding of these two young things. For how, she asked herself, could they at their age really be expected to comprehend that a woman (their mother at that) of her age might still be young enough to fall in love—to feel the fever and passion of youth all over again (as she felt it for Robert Tracy). To them it must seem incredible—perhaps even disgraceful.

Pat spoke now . . . scratching his thick curls.

"I say . . . Mum . . . look here . . . have we been so neglectful of you . . . left you alone too much? I couldn't help being called up, or you know I'd have stayed here with you."

"Oh, I *know*, my darling!" exclaimed his mother.

"And I had to get a job. I couldn't live on you, could I?" put in Judy, brows drawn fiercely together. And added: "But I'm here every night. I never dreamed you'd want to put someone in Daddy's shoes. He was so terrific . . . you *couldn't* have met any man as good . . . even half as wonderful."

Mrs. Green's forehead felt damp. She trembled a little. Fighting between her love for her children and her newly awakened passionate love for Robert Tracy. She wished with all her heart that Judy liked Robert. Katherine *knew* about the hostility between those two. It made her position so much harder.

Judy was saying:

"So that's why you've been so funny lately. I was wondering. I met Pat in town specially to tell him I was worried. I thought you might be ill or something. I might have spared myself the trouble. It's this. You . . . you're not content with us, and you're going to bring someone else to the cottage, into our lives. Oh, it'll be *hateful* . . ."

"Wait a moment, Ju!" put in Pat. "No use flying off the handle. If Mummy wants to get married again, I suppose it's her right. It's a bit selfish of us to sit on the idea and refuse to wish her luck."

Katherine Green threw him a passionately grateful look. Her darling, considerate Pat. He *would* be the one to try at least to see things from her point of view, bless him. But Judy, with stormy, resentful gaze, said:

"Who's the chap, anyhow, Mummy? Do we know him?"

Katherine Green's thin, tired face was quite white now. She thought: *"How is it possible they have been so blind? Not to know it's Robert. Robert, who is always over here and so good to me. To all of us. Robert, who has been my right hand for years. In love with me for years. And I've said 'no' so many, many times because I wouldn't put anybody in David's place. Because I felt the children needed all my love and attention. But now Judy is grown up, working . . . and Pat a soldier . . . probably off at any moment on foreign service . . . I realize how alone I've been . . . how tired of working and planning and living from day to day, year to year, without a shoulder to lean on . . . someone strong and fine and calm, like Robert. I realize how fast my heart can still beat when Robert's arms hold me . . . when his lips touch mine . . . oh, why couldn't the children have guessed . . . understood . . . been ready to help and encourage me?"*

But she knew, as she stood there, under the accusing gaze of her young son and daughter, that it had been too much to expect. She had spoiled them always. They had become fiercely possessive, just as they were fiercely devoted to her. Poor, loyal young things . . . why should she ever have expected them to sympathize when their mother confessed to a need of a new love . . . *another kind of love?*

She began to express some of these thoughts aloud . . . in halting, stumbling speech . . . her eyes beseeching them. They listened, silent and disapproving . . . even though Pat wanted to sympathize, was always less violent in his emotions than Judy.

Judy suddenly interrupted her mother's explanations:

"Well, I think it's *awful* . . . that we shouldn't have been enough for you and that you should want to spoil everything by bringing a stranger into our midst."

Katherine, suddenly irritated, exclaimed:

"Darling, what nonsense! Don't be dramatic. And anyhow I shall go and live in my new husband's house . . . not he in mine."

Judy caught her breath.

"So you'll be walking out on us."

"Judy, why must you put everything in such an unattractive light? I shan't 'walk out' on you. You'll both have a home with us. . . . With Robert and me."

"Robert——" Judy caught her up on the name. "Robert ——Oh, for heaven's *sake*, don't say you're going to marry *Uncle Robert* . . . from Cooltye Farm! . . ."

Katherine's ash-blonde head went a little higher, proudly, even though her eyes were scared, and her heart was pounding.

"Yes, I'm going to marry him," she said. "I know you've got a 'thing' about him, Judy, but he's a very fine person, I think even Pat will admit that . . . and he has always been a real friend to us all. He takes an enormous interest in both of you. He offers you Cooltye Farm as a home and says you will always be welcome in it. Regard him as a friend, if not as a father."

Silence. A miserable silence for Katherine Green. It was so eloquent of the shock and concern that her two cherished children were feeling. Pat mumbled:

"Oh, lord. Uncle Bob! Never twigged that one. Of course we might have guessed. Only just never dreamt you'd want to get married again, Mum."

She caught his arm.

"Pat, darling, is it so awful? Isn't it natural of me to want a . . . a husband? I'd never actually try to put Robert in Daddy's shoes. Don't think of it that way. Daddy had his own niche. He was *Daddy* . . . your father. But Robert will have *his* place in my life. Do you see? And when you and Ju are married you'll both be so glad I've got someone nice to take care of me."

"I s'pose so," muttered Pat.

He felt a sudden new jealousy of Robert Tracy. He was a good chap and all that . . . as an uncle. But as a *stepfather*! Pat wrinkled his nose. Lordy! What a thought! He might try to interfere with his personal affairs. As for Mum becoming Mrs. Tracy and living in Cooltye Farm. That idea upset Pat not a little. Awful to think of their own home breaking up . . . the happy little trio here at the cottage disintegrating. And Mum . . . in Uncle Robert's home . . . Uncle Robert's arms. Pat's cheeks burned and he lit a cigarette hurriedly, forgetting his new resolve to "cut down smokes." He did not feel angry with his mother. Only disappointed that things could not have remained as they were.

But Judy flamed into sudden hot revolt.

"Of all men in the world . . . Uncle Robert . . . to make *him* our stepfather . . . when you know I could never be fond of him! To put *him* in Daddy's place and leave us for *him*! I'll never get over it!" Her voice rose and she crossed her arms on her chest and tossed a mass of burnt coppery hair out of her eyes, eyes flashing at her mother.

Mrs. Green protested:

"Judy darling . . . it's all so silly . . . your animosity towards Robert. He's so ready to be friendly with you."

"Well, I shall never act like a loving stepdaughter to him, I promise you, Mummy. Never. I won't even live at Cooltye Farm, either. If my home goes, *I go with it*."

The colour now rushed into Katherine Green's cheeks, and the tempo of her heart increased considerably.

"Oh, *Judy*!"

Pat flung an embarrassed look at his mother, then muttered: "Hold your horses, Ju."

She turned on him like a young tigress.

"Are *you* going to be so disloyal to Daddy's memory as to accept Robert Tracy in his place? Are you going to go and live at Cooltye Farm when he's master there, and accept *his* domination?"

Pat chewed his lips, scarlet to the ears. He was torn between his love and loyalty to his mother and his own bitter disappointment in her news. Most certainly he didn't want even Uncle Robert chucking orders at him. He had always appreciated the sort of freedom a fellow had living with Mum. He was imaginative and could quickly conjure up fearful visions of Robert Tracy telling him to do this or that, and

21

expecting some sort of "stepfilial" response. As for picturing him in intimate relationship with Mum . . . that was altogether distasteful to the young man.

Katherine felt the last ounce of fight go out of her as she saw what lay on her son's frank countenance. He had always been transparent and incapable of hiding his feelings. So *he*, too, was against this marriage and was going to side with Judy. This suspicion was not much allayed when he said:

"Well, I don't suppose it's my business whether Mother marries again or not, but I certainly shan't want to live at Cooltye Farm. I could never regard it as my home. Just as well I shall be posted abroad in the near future. Probably to Korea."

Katherine turned white. Those words were like a knife in her heart. She felt incapable of further speech or action. Then Judy, very tight-lipped, placed the Corgi on the floor, brushed her skirt and turned towards the door.

"Let's go down to the garage, Pat," she said in a choked voice. "I need fresh air."

Katherine Green shut her eyes as though trying to get a grip on herself. When she opened them again her young son and daughter had gone. She looked through a haze at the remains of the tea-party which had started off so gaily. The room was very quiet except for the ticking of the cuckoo clock. That clock had belonged to her father-in-law. David had always cherished it. She could see him even now winding it up before he went to bed. With much of Pat's schoolboy humour and sweetness in him, grown man though he was, the little cuckoo clock had never failed to amuse Dr. Green. She could see him this moment turning the key, and then looking over his shoulder at her with a smile.

"Come to bed, Sleepy Head," he would say.

He had loved her and she had loved him. His early death had been an appalling blow, shattering her little world. She had only lived through the intolerable pain of that loss because of the children. And as she had just told them, her whole life had been devoted to their upbringing—divided between domestic routine and her writing. During the war, when they had been small, she had known further privation and a fear that was only for *them*. The sky above peaceful little Cooltye had often been dark with the shadow of German bombers. She had wondered sometimes what kind of a world she had brought her children into. The end of war had meant a certain amount of relaxation, and she had started to make a regular income out of her children's books. She had managed to send Judy to a fine school, and Pat to Shrewsbury, where his father had been before him.

All of her life had been one vast effort for them. Throughout it she had been alone. She had been an orphan when David married her and did not even remember her own parents. The uncle and aunt who had brought her up were dead. David, too, had been extraordinarily lacking in relations, with only one brother in Australia, who wrote to her at intervals, but who had never helped her much. No . . . the only real help and advice she had ever received was from Robert Tracy. He had bought Cooltye Farm soon after the war, after his demobilization from the Navy, in which he had served as a volunteer. He had come out of that sacrifice with one lung affected, but an open-air life had saved him and he was now strong and well again. They had made friends the moment they met, which was in the village hall. He had been on a local committee and she serving at a stall for some Red Cross bazaar. And later, when his feelings had changed from mere friendship to a passionate love, she had refused him—at first because she had thought never to replace David. Later, when she had grown to lean upon him more and more and to want him as a lover as well as a friend, she had said "no" solely because she thought that the children would not want a stepfather.

How right she had been!

For a moment Katherine stood with her face hidden in her hands—full of torment. Last weekend, while Judy was out with friends, Robert had come over here and they had had a "showdown." He had said:

"I won't let you say 'no' any more. You've done enough for the children. You owe something to yourself. You've got to marry me, Katherine. You've *got to*, my darling."

And suddenly she had surrendered and felt a great load

being removed from her shoulders. The woman of forty odd had slipped back to girlhood, thrilled and enchanted, listening to all his plans for their future. She had realized how marvellous it would be to say good-bye to widowhood and that loneliness which even the children had not been able to dispel after David died. Marvellous to have a man at her side again, ready to relieve her of so many responsibilities.

Robert had a prosperous farm and a small but useful private income. At the present moment he had a daily woman at Cooltye, but after their marriage he had said he would get a married couple—the woman to cook and the man for gardening.

"You've spent enough time at the kitchen sink, as well as at your typewriter," he said firmly. "You're going to have a little rest once you're my wife."

And he had been so sweet about the children. Making more plans to help find a suitable career for Pat after he left the Army and to do something for Judy. Katherine felt a sudden wave of resentment at the memory of their rigid, unkind acceptance of her news. They hadn't been fair to Robert. They hadn't given him a chance.

But if her marriage was going to cause all this distress and drive those two out of her life . . . she could not . . . would not marry Robert. No matter what it cost her to give him up.

There came the sound of a car. Katherine Green knew that engine . . . Robert Tracy's old Ford (he planned to sell it and buy a new Standard for her as a wedding present). She saw, through the windows, the tall, loose-limbed figure of Robert getting out of his car. He had a box in one hand. She remembered that he had said he would bring over some eggs and have a word with the children. He had been a bit nervous about the way in which they might receive him once they knew . . . although he had tried not to show it. Poor Robert! He wanted so badly to put the right foot forward.

Katherine rushed into her bedroom, wiped her face, which was wet with tears, and hastily powdered it. She had never felt so utterly lost and miserable.

She heard Robert's voice.

"Are you there? Anybody in?"

She advanced slowly into the sitting-room.

The moment Robert Tracy saw her he knew that everything had gone wrong. He took the pipe hastily from his mouth and put it in the pocket of the old flannel coat he was wearing.

"Haven't the kids turned up yet?" he asked hopefully.

"Sit down, Robert," she said. "I'm afraid I haven't got very good news."

He would not sit. He remained standing, and so did she. In a halting voice she told him exactly what had been said by Judy and Pat. She finished:

"It'll never work, Robert. They've had me to themselves too long. They were just appalled at the thought of my marrying again. I can't do it . . . you must forgive me and try to understand."

He was silent a moment. His gaze had never left her face. He could see that she had been crying and that she looked utterly dejected. An intense anger seized him. Anger against those two selfish young things who had caused her this misery. One had to make excuses for them, but damn it . . . it was sheer crass egotism on their parts. *They* wanted to keep their mother to themselves. Yes . . . extract more and more from her in the way of sacrifice and devotion, and then, when they themselves chose to marry, they'd push off and leave her quite alone. And she was prepared to make more sacrifices. She was like that. He knew of no finer mother. But she was also a very attractive woman . . . and the woman he loved. With all his being he loved Katherine Green. He had been a confirmed bachelor until he met her. They had so much in common. Apart from her physical attraction . . . for to him she was a most beautiful person . . . she had brains. She read a lot, and so did he, in the evenings, after his work on the farm was finished. They both shared a strong devotion to Sussex and the Downs, and liked long country walks. They were perfect friends, and as husband and wife he believed that they would be entirely fulfilled. He was not going to let two thoughtless, selfish young people like Judy and Pat (Judy in particular was difficult . . . Pat might be all right) rob her of her right to happiness now.

He walked up to Katherine and quietly took her in his arms. "I was afraid it might be like this," he said. "But you're

25

wrong if you think it's going to end here. It isn't. One has to fight for everything in life, Katherine, and we're going to fight for our marriage. You're absolutely wrong if you think I'm going to give you up."

The hot tears gushed to her eyes. It was such heaven to feel his warm, strong embrace again. For an instant she surrendered to it, and looked through that haze of tears at the face which had grown so very dear to her. Robert was not particularly handsome, except for his fine physique and bright hazel eyes which were full of humour and intelligence. He was a little too thin and bony, with a high bridge to his nose and jutting-out brows. He was essentially a man's man. At home with animals, a gun, a fishing-rod. He was capable of great kindliness and generosity. Never had she known a more generous man. Not only to herself, whom he loved, but to everybody in Cooltye. He was the most popular farmer in the district. And he had been popular in the Navy. She knew that. So many of his old Naval friends came down to the farm to see him or wrote to him from far-off lands. And he had loved the sea. But his heart was really in the land and he had wanted to be a farmer from the time that he took an agricultural degree up at Cambridge, twenty years ago.

She liked so many things about Robert. Not only his integral character, but his strong, well-shaped hands, and his dark, springy hair, only now beginning to thin at the temples. The sensitiveness of his lips; the mahogany brownness of his skin. So essentially a man who was out in all weathers. But there was nothing rough or uncouth about him. He was fastidious about cleanliness and order. She could not have borne to share life at Cooltye Farm with Robert unless he had that orderly side. For Katherine Green hated anything slovenly.

In few ways did he resemble David, her first love. He had been extremely good-looking and of slender build, and had much more of the boy in him. Robert Tracy was, at forty-two, old and rather set in his ways. But she liked that "oldness." She needed it. She had spent so much time looking after the young. She wanted now to have someone strong and decisive who could take care of *her*.

Just for a moment she gave herself up to the luxury of loving and wanting Robert, her slim fingers playing with his thick hair. Then she drew back and shook her head.

"No, Robert, let me go . . . don't tempt me. I can't marry you. Not if Pat and Judy feel this way about it."

3

To be torn between the man you love and want to marry and the children whom you love equally in quite another way is no enviable position for any woman. And it was the position in which Katherine Green found herself—and suffered accordingly. After Judy had stormed out of the cottage, followed by an embarrassed Pat, even while Katherine's sensibilities for her children were acutely awake and listening for them to come back, the rest of her was all Robert's. She sat beside him on the sofa in the warm stillness of that golden summer evening and tried to do as he bade her. To relax. To think of herself rather than of her children, and to remember that today was not for ever.

During the last hour Robert had been arguing with her—trying to show her what to do.

"Time doesn't stand still, you know, Kath," he reminded her. "And the children are no longer little things, entirely dependent on their mother. They are adults. Pat is a soldier. Judy works for her living. They don't need you in the same way they used to do, although I suppose it is hard for you to realize that because for so many years you have been their backbone and support."

Flushed and puzzle-eyed, Katherine looked at him, winding her fingers agitatedly together. With deep affection and understanding Robert Tracy read all the doubts and anxieties in those eyes which were still as beautiful and limpid as a girl's. And he watched the nervous hands and thought that they, too, were beautiful, although she so often decried them —ruefully remarking that once they had been as slender as Judy's, with long, polished nails. Years of hard work on her typewriter had changed all that. These days she kept those nails filed short. Continual work at the kitchen sink or washtub had made them rough and enlarged the knuckles. But to Robert they were strong, brave hands, and he liked to kiss them. He took them now and brushed them with his lips, smiling almost as he would have done at a bewildered child.

"Sometimes I don't think you're as old or wise as your own daughter," he teased her. "If that young woman wants anything she gets it—or will do—as you'll see. She's got a touch of ruthlessness. You're such a generous creature, Katherine. I adore your generosity, but I think you, too, should be a little harder. You'll get nowhere if you let yourself be put upon, and remember that you've done everything on earth for those two since their father died. Isn't it time *you* had a break?"

She bit her lip.

"I have thought so sometimes, Rob, and that's why I agreed to marry you. But . . ."

"And do you still love me and still want to marry me?" he broke in.

She tried to draw her hands away, but he kept them imprisoned.

"Go on . . . face up to the truth. Even if it's against your maternal instincts to admit it—do you still love me and want to marry me, Katherine?"

"Of course I do," she said almost crossly. "One can't change one's mind overnight about a man. I shall never love anybody else. Of that I'm quite convinced."

His face cleared.

"Then that's settled. You're going to marry me, my dear."

"But, Robert, you saw the way the children reacted to my announcement."

Robert Tracy's firm mouth tightened a shade more.

"Did you think that to be admired? Were you edified by such a display of crass selfishness?"

Quick to defend her children, Katherine cried:

"It was a shock to them, Rob! It *must* have been. Perhaps I have been wrong to keep our growing love for each other so to myself . . . I ought to have confided in them before and told them that I was falling in love with you."

He put his tongue in his cheek.

"That, my sweet Katherine, would merely have given

young Judy an earlier chance to try and make you refuse me."

"It's so unfortunate that you and Judy don't get on very well. Pat wasn't too bad about it. Darling Pat . . . he's so soft-hearted . . . I'm sure it wouldn't take much for you to make an ally of *him*."

"Your son is more like you, my dear."

"Oh, I don't know where Judy gets that hard streak!" cried Katherine helplessly. "Heaven knows her father was the kindest and most understanding of men."

"Well, never mind where she gets it. As I say, it's not a bad streak for a girl to possess. It's a hard world, Katherine, for the young today. And they daren't be too soft and sentimental."

She looked at him with glistening eyes.

"I think you understand youth even better than I do . . . it's such a tragedy that Judy doesn't ever try to talk to you and learn what a wonderful person you are."

He bent and touched her lips with his.

"I love you so much, my darling Katherine. And I just can't sit back and see you do all the struggling and fighting any more. You've got to marry me and come and live at the Farm, and let me look after you for ever and ever. As for the kids . . . it'll be their home as well and I'll do everything I can to make Judy less antagonistic."

Her heart began to beat with fresh hope for the future. She had felt so utterly crushed by the manner in which her young daughter had taken the announcement of her engagement to Robert. She had so *wanted* all of them to be happy together. And she *was* tired. She had been without love and fulfilment for such a long time. She could think of nothing more heavenly than life at Cooltye Farm—and Robert as a companion. She did not doubt that he would do his best with the children, otherwise she could never have entertained the thought of giving the children a stepfather. Never, never could any woman doubt Robert Tracy's integrity and goodness of heart.

"Oh! If only I thought it would be a success!" she cried.

"We'll make it so, Kath . . . you and I together. Don't let Judy's attitude today discolour the whole affair. Keep a sense of proportion, darling. If it has been a shock, Judy will get over it. And quite honestly you ought to be angry with her for not being more sympathetic and unselfish towards the mother to whom she owes so much. Yet here you are, contemplating further sacrifice. You can overdo mother-love, my sweet. It isn't good for young Judy—or Pat—to think they can always have all their own way."

She sighed.

"I expect you're right."

"And I want you to look ahead," he added gently. "I swear I am not only saying this because I want you so much myself . . . I'd say it if you were contemplating marriage with another chap. . . . Those two will marry and leave *you* in the not-so-distant future; then you'll be quite alone. Oughtn't they to have thought of that before denouncing your wish to marry again? And oughtn't *you* to remember that it won't be so easy for you in the fifties and sixties to live *quite alone*?"

She knew that every word he said was right and logical. Of course Judy and Pat would eventually marry and leave her—without any compunction. She began to feel a little resentful that Judy hadn't shown more consideration for her. And suddenly her mind was made up again. She rose and, with hot cheeks and flashing eyes, announced her final decision:

"You're absolutely right. We'll carry on, Rob. I won't be bullied out of my marriage by Judy or anybody in the world."

Robert Tracy gained his feet. His own pulses thrilled. He thought he had never seen her look more beautiful, and he was immeasurably thrilled by the knowledge that she had chosen him. He knew how much those two young people meant to her.

He took her in his arms, and held her close, his cheek pressed against hers.

"You'll never regret it, Kath. I'll do my damnedest to make you a good husband, darling, and I swear as I've sworn before that I'll consider it my solemn duty to share your affection and concern for Judy and Pat."

She said no more but yielded to his long kiss, conscious of immense relief that she had been guided back into the haven of this man's love. For an hour or two this evening she had felt like a rudderless ship tossing in an impossibly rough sea.

"And I'll swear to do my best to make you happy, Rob darling, and not to be too stupidly sentimental about my children," she said.

"I think your devotion to them is rather touching," he said. "And I wouldn't have it otherwise. Just keep it all in perspective, sweet, and don't be the one to take all the raps."

She was about to answer, but paused; she had heard the dogs barking.

"Oh, dear," she breathed, glancing out of the casements. "Here they come, back."

Robert gripped her hand and held it in a vice.

"Courage, and no drawing back now, Katherine."

She pursed her lips and then laughed, and smoothed back her tumbled hair.

"All right. I'll be brave."

Brother and sister walked into the cottage followed by the two Corgis, who rushed across the room, fawned upon Katherine, then pushed open the door communicating with the kitchen and attacked their drinking-bowls thirstily.

With fast-beating heart Katherine looked at her children. They avoided her gaze. They looked very hot as though they had been walking a long way. Pat muttered:

"'Evening, sir," to Robert, and then walked across the room and switched on the radio.

Judy was barely civil.

"I am going up to have a bath," she announced in a rather defiant voice.

She was in one of her worst moods. She was not only exhausted by the walk which she had just taken, but by her own youthful, turbulent emotions. It was anathema to her to see Robert Tracy standing there holding her mother by the arm in that possessive way. Quite irrationally she hated him, although she knew in her heart of hearts that he was the nicest man and the best friend her mother had ever had. But in her eyes he was about to take her mother away from her and break up their home. He had even come between her and her brother, she told herself childishly, because she and Pat had never really quarrelled seriously (beyond some childish dispute) until this afternoon. And then Pat had ticked her off because, he had said, she hadn't given "Mum" a break.

"I don't want a stepfather any more than you do, but I think you ought to be decent to Mum about it. After all, it's her life, and if she wants to marry again it's hardly fair of us to try and stop it."

Judy, with complete egotism, had stormed at him.

Why should Mummy marry again? She had reached this age without wanting to replace Daddy. Why couldn't she go on with just Pat and herself? It was perfectly beastly to think of giving up the little cottage and all of them going to Cooltye Farm and having to toe the line to Robert Tracy.

"Mummy won't be *ours* any more! She'll be Mrs. Tracy. Everything will be changed. It will be absolutely hateful!"

Pat had agreed with this but, with more thought for his mother, tried to argue Judy into rationalizing the thing.

"You've got a job, and now I'm away I expect Mum's feeling a bit lonely."

That had brought a fresh storm from Judy. It was all very well for Pat. Yes, he was a man and in the Army now. It didn't mean so much to him. He didn't live here any more. It was *her* mother Robert Tracy was taking away and *her* home. Nothing would induce her to stay on in the village and knuckle down to life in Cooltye Farm, meekly, with a stepfather. Uncle Robert was quite all right in his way, but it would mean she would never have Mummy to herself again. They would always be holding hands and she would turn into the "odd man out."

"Nothing will induce me to play 'gooseberry' and I think it's frightfully selfish of Mummy to take everything away from us and give it all to Uncle Robert."

Further argument had followed. Pat, partly on his sister's side, but mostly defending his mother's right to live her own life and re-marry if she so wished. He had assured Judy that he was not at all pleased about it, but begged her to be reasonable.

Then Judy had lost her temper and accused him of being "weak," and doing anything for peace's sake. Whereupon Pat had dried up and they had completed their walk in stony silence.

Judy was now the most unhappy girl in the world—
wrapped in a cloak of egotistical misery and the self-pity such
as can only be felt by the very young who feel their wrongs
so intensely, shutting themselves out from the rest of the
world. And she made Robert Tracy the scapegoat, the ogre
responsible for her despair.

She did not want to speak to him. But her mother's voice,
clear and rather cool, called her back from the doorway.

"Don't go upstairs for a moment, Judy. I'd like you two
to come and offer Uncle Robert and myself your congratulations."

Pat, flushing, immediately complied with this request,
and he switched off the wireless again.

"Best wishes and all that," he mumbled.

"Thanks, darling," his mother said gratefully.

Robert Tracy gave the lad a friendly smile.

"Thank you, Pat. I'll do my best for your mother. You
know that, old boy. And I don't want anything in our particular relationship to change. I shan't attempt the 'big stepfather' act, you know."

Pat gave an awkward laugh. He could not pretend that
he found this situation to his liking. Judy was right when she
said that Mum's marrying again subtly but quite definitely
would break up the happy home, and set a gulf between them
which might be difficult to bridge. At the same time the boy
had always liked Robert Tracy—even admired him. It was
not as though his mother was marrying some frightful cad
not to be tolerated at any price. Judy was being absurd. But
he hated any quarrel with her. They had always been so
close.

Katherine Green stood tensely, gaze fixed on her young
daughter, waiting for Judy to say something to ease the situation and draw them together again. And her heart sank
as she saw her daughter's face. It had a granite look. Quite a
frighteningly hard expression for one so young. She knew
from experience that there was a very stubborn streak in
Judy.

"Well, darling," Katherine said gently. "Won't you offer
Uncle Robert and me your good wishes?"

Judy looked from her mother to the tall man beside her.

She felt her whole body trembling with rage because those two stood there with linked arms. Linked against *her*, she thought. They would always be linked in future and always be against her. She said:

"Oh, of course, all the best. But please don't ask me to take any part in the celebrations. Nor to go on living in Cooltye. As a matter of fact my friend Elizabeth wants me to take a job in London, and I expect I shall now, and go and live up there in digs. So you won't be bothered with me at all."

Robert Tracy felt Katherine's arm quiver. He knew that she had been struck a blow and was flinching under it. But he drew her arm even closer, trying to give her some of his strength. The silly child, he thought angrily, not to realize what a lot this meant to her mother, and to be more gracious, after all that had been done for *her*.

He tried to introduce a light note, rather than allow heavy drama to evolve from the situation.

"You aren't afraid I am going to be a cruel stepfather, are you, Judy?" he laughed. "As I said to Pat . . . I don't want my marriage with your mother to alter our old relationship at all, my dear. Just look on me as a friend, and I suggest we might drop the 'Uncle' in future and that you both call me Robert."

She gave him a frigid stare.

"Thanks. But as I say, Cooltye won't be seeing much more of *me*."

Katherine, her heart beating hard with agitation, threw her daughter a beseeching glance.

"Judy darling, there's no need to do anything drastic like that, surely! I should hate you to leave home and—"

"Our home will be breaking up in any case," broke in Judy unsmilingly.

Robert put in:

"I am most anxious that you should find a new one under my roof, Judy. I'd like to have you do up one of the rooms to suit yourself, and—"

Now she interrupted him:

"Thanks, but I wouldn't dream of living with you and my mother. I'm sure you'll both prefer to be alone."

Now Katherine moved away from her future husband and came up to her daughter, and caught her hand.

"Judy darling, *please* . . . don't take it like this!"

For a moment the girl longed to throw herself into her mother's arms. In reality she loved her better than anybody in the world, but she could not make it an unselfish love. It was greedy and selfish. She wanted at this very moment to push Robert Tracy out of the cottage and weep bitterly on her mother's shoulder. Instead she resorted to further hardness, and a lack of grace which held none of the sweet laughing Judy who had walked into this cottage earlier this afternoon.

"Oh, it's your life and not mine, my dear Mummy. I'm not dictating to you and I hope you won't dictate to me," she said. "And if I don't want a stepfather . . . I'm sorry, and it's just too bad. But I *don't*. I shan't stay in Cooltye. And *please* don't ask me to come to the wedding, either. . . ."

Her voice broke. She turned her gaze from her mother's stricken face, tore her hand away, and rushed out of the room.

Robert Tracy gave a sharp, exasperated sigh. So Judy meant war, and there was nothing for the moment that he could do about it. He felt no sense of personal injury. And he thought he understood—the silly child was just mad with jealousy! But he felt deeply the hurt that she had given Katherine. He could not bear to see that look on his dear love's face or to feel partly responsible for the fast-gathering shadows in this little home. Angrily, he told himself that he would not allow Judy to make him feel that *he* had destroyed their peace. Katherine needed him as much as he needed her and would need him still more as she got older and less able to work.

Pat pulled at the lobe of a crimson ear and muttered an excuse about going to change.

"See you later, Mum. All the best again, Uncle . . . I mean Robert."

Silence fell between Katherine and Robert once they were alone. Then Katherine said in a strangled voice:

"Pat's been an angel to take it like this . . . but he *would*."

36

"Don't worry too much about Judy. She'll come round in time." Robert tried to soothe her.

Katherine's lips quivered.

He walked up to her and hugged her closely.

"Please, please don't be unhappy. I know it'll be all right in the long run. It's all a question of time, my darling."

She relaxed in his embrace for a moment.

"Oh, don't worry . . . I'm not going to rescind anything I've said to you, Rob. But it breaks my heart to see Judy so . . . so hostile. And she's so young. I couldn't bear her to go to live alone in London and be without a home or mother."

"She won't. It was only a childish threat. I bet you'll talk her round after I've gone, and she'll have a good cry and get over it," said Robert with a slight laugh.

But Katherine wondered . . . wondered miserably whether Robert was right, and whether he knew quite as well as she did how stubborn Judy could be.

"Don't ask me to come to the wedding!" Those harsh words echoed in her ears, filling her with dismay.

To have a wedding and not have Judy there . . . that would be too awful to contemplate. She couldn't mean it . . . she *mustn't*. Robert was right, thought Katherine feverishly, she must talk her round tonight and put things right between them again.

4

KATHERINE GREEN was nothing if not a tactful woman. She decided after Robert had gone that perhaps tonight was not the time for a "showdown" with her young daughter. Better leave her to get over her present irrational mood, then tackle her again.

Judy was a little surprised, perhaps, and secretly admiring when Katherine made no further mention of her engagement to Robert that evening.

During supper the mother put up a show of nonchalance which cost her more than either of her children guessed. She was even gay. Talked about them—not herself—and cleverly lured Pat into telling them about his Army life. So, over a meal of cold bacon and salad and a bottle of beer, Pat related some quite amusing anecdotes about his Unit which made even Judy smile. Brother and sister took their cue from Katherine.

There was no animosity—no reference to their flareup during the walk home. Anybody who didn't know the facts would have thought these three as united and happy as before.

But all the time Katherine was anxiously wondering what lay behind Judy's stubborn little mask of a face, anxiously praying that she had not done the wrong thing for *them* by accepting Robert, which was only an advancement of her own happiness. And yet was it "only"? If the children were sensible they would benefit by having a grand man like Robert for a stepfather. He was a prosperous farmer and a cultured man with a lovely old home. He would not be ungenerous to them. They would really have a far superior home to this tiny cottage in which they had all had a struggle to live well—

and maintain the degree of education and comfort that their father would have wished for them.

Judy nervously avoided her mother's gaze while they chatted together, but she took the trouble to ask how the new book was getting on—if Mummy had done any writing while she was in town today.

Katherine announced that she had finished two chapters of her new story book for tiny tots.

"I'm introducing a new character," she said, as she leaned back and allowed her son to hold his lighter for her after-supper cigarette. *"Lionel the Lizard.* Do you remember the tame lizard you used to have when you were about ten, Judy, and how you adored it? I think I shall have to dedicate the book to you, darling."

"Oh, what fun!" Judy said absently.

"My goodness, Mum, you are full of endless ideas, I must say!" exclaimed Pat.

Then silence fell. Katherine was thinking:

"It's been hard finding new ideas lately . . . getting harder with every year to be original. Thank goodness I won't have to stick at it quite so hard once I am Robert's wife. I can sit back and let him support me and just make enough out of my writing to go on giving the children their allowance and make them feel independent."

Judy's thoughts were embittered:

"I suppose she did love me when I was a little girl—she was always frightfully good about letting me have pets—understanding what I wanted. But things seem to have changed since I grew up. She doesn't understand me at all now. Otherwise she wouldn't have expected me to throw myself into Uncle Robert's arms and say how wonderful to have him as a stepfather. I don't want him; I'll never want him . . . never."

The boy's thoughts were more simple, if a trifle gloomy:

"What a wizard Mum is, the way she does things! I'm a darned lucky guy, when I think of that chap at the camp who told me he avoids going home for leaves and pushes off on his own because his Mum nags him and the rest of the family all day. He isn't even allowed to smoke in the house. Mum's never nagged. But I wish this little place wasn't busting up.

It won't be the same, going back to Cooltye Farm, even though it's a darned nice place."

The meal over, Katherine said:

"Judy, you look tired—go and rest, darling. And you probably want to go down to the Spread Eagle to play darts, don't you, Pat?"

Judy gave a tight-lipped smile.

"Oh, I'll help you wash up, Mummy."

"I'll help, too," seconded Pat, in the act of lighting his pipe.

But Katherine refused to allow it. They both knew when she was adamant, and she shut the kitchen door on them. They could hear the splash of water and the clatter of dishes.

Pat eyed his sister with a frown.

"I say, Judy, we can't go on being strung up over this affair. Oughn't you to make the peace with Mum?"

"I can't . . . we're all very pleasant outwardly, anyhow."

"Well, personally I found supper pretty grim, and you can see *she's* under a strain."

Judy tossed her head.

"Aren't we all? It's not my fault, is it?"

"Oh, hang it, Ju, we got all worked up during our walk, but it's darned stupid. Let's discuss things in a friendly way. I don't really think we ought to make *her* miserable, as she seems bent on this marriage."

A quick intake of breath from Judy.

"Must we go through it all again? Really, Pat, I got back my self-control during my bath, and I don't want to lose it again. This thing has hit me much more than it has you. I live at home, and you don't."

He threw her a sympathetic glance.

"I realize it is tough on you, but old Robert's a decent chap, really, and we've got to look at things from Mum's point of view as well as our own."

"I'm sorry, I can't," said Judy, her cheeks burning. "I just *can't*. And I mean it when I say I'm going to quit Cooltye and take a job with Elizabeth. And now if you want to go down to the Spread Eagle, carry on. I want to write to Tony and tell him that he will be seeing more of me in the future than he thinks as I'm going to live in town."

Which was precisely what she informed her mother when eventually Katherine summoned up some more courage to speak openly to Judy. It was on the following morning, Sunday. Pat was still asleep, having what he called his "lie in." It had done the mother's heart good when she had passed his open door (Pat always slept with doors and windows wide open in what she thought a "hurricane") to see him lying there, one hand under his brown cheek, curly chestnut mop against the pillow, looking so young—so innocent, for all the world as though he were still her small boy rather than the fledgling soldier. She went downstairs to make breakfast—an ache in her heart. A pity, she reflected, that children had to grow up. They were so sweet, so cuddlesome, when they were babies. Things might have been easier if she had married Robert ten years ago while she was still a very young widow. The children, when small, would have accepted Robert as a matter of course, and very quickly got over their first jealousy.

She walked into the kitchen and was surprised to find Judy there, already dressed in linen slacks and shirt, eating her breakfast—she had never before known Judy to get up on a Sunday morning. She, too, liked a long "lie." Katherine said:

"Good morning, darling. You've been very quiet. I didn't hear a sound . . . I thought you were still in bed."

Judy looked ill at ease, and glanced at her plate.

"I couldn't sleep, so I thought I'd get up and get *your* breakfast for a change. I was just going to do it and bring it up. I thought *you* were still asleep."

Katherine's heart warmed to her young daughter. How fresh and pretty she looked! Like the dewy summer morning —one of those roses out there on the spangled lawn. The sky was a miraculous blue, and the birds singing madly. A faint mist hung over the woods in the distance. It was going to be a glorious hot day. If only things could be as they used to be, Katherine thought. They could all pack up a picnic lunch and go off somewhere—on the Downs, maybe. She longed to make things right between herself and Judy. And she was touched by the thought that Judy had meant to take up her breakfast. But Judy immediately spoiled things by saying:

"I want to be early, anyhow, as I've got to do a lot of sorting and packing. I'll pay you, Mummy, but if you don't mind I must put a trunk call through to Elizabeth Chapman and tell her that I am going up to town when Pat goes back to his Unit . . . on Tuesday. That'll give her time to find me a room on Monday. There's such a muck in my room it'll take ages to find what I want to keep and what I want to leave behind. If you don't mind I'll store a lot of stuff down here until I'm more settled."

At once Katherine Green felt the world being cut from under her feet again. All the hopes she had entertained that everything would be all right this morning faded. Judy stood up, looking straight and determined.

"I'll put the kettle and toaster on for you, Mummy," she said quite amiably.

But behind that amiability the older woman could read all the animosity and bitterness that must have been festering in the girl's heart during the night.

Katherine braced herself and made an effort to conquer Judy as well as her own doubts about the future. (Those doubts did not exist apart from Judy, who seemed to have the knack of making her feel that she was doing her young daughter a frightful wrong by marrying Robert Tracy).

"Leave my toast a moment, Ju darling. I'll have a 'cuppa' out of your pot. Sit down and let's talk things over quietly, without any ill feeling on either side."

Judy shrugged her shoulders and reseated herself.

"Oh, I have no ill feelings, Mummy. In fact, I feel rather dead inside. I just don't want to live at Cooltye Farm when you move, that's all."

"Oh, Judy, don't talk about feeling 'dead.' You make it sound so terrible!" cried her mother, flushed and distressed.

"Sorry. I can't help it. I'm not like Pat, I suppose. He's taken it more calmly, although I know he feels it just as much as I do. But he doesn't have to live at home, and he can spend his leaves at Cooltye Farm just as well as at the cottage. Besides, he may go abroad, anyhow."

"But, Judy, you talk of packing up and going away when Pat goes the day after tomorrow. Why? I don't expect to get married or leave here until the end of the summer."

Judy's eyes narrowed.

"Oh, I dare say you will. I dare say Uncle Robert will speed things up. And I might just as well get myself settled. I shall go and see them at the Dower House this afternoon and explain what's happened."

Katherine's heart began to jerk more in anger now than grief.

"So you're going to let the whole village know that you're walking out on me because I am getting married again?"

Judy's cheeks reddened. She muttered:

"Oh, I don't need to do that. I can just say circumstances have altered so that I've *got* to live in London. But I dare say the whole of Cooltye knows, anyhow. Pat and I are the only ones who didn't guess."

"You are bent on making me feel a criminal because I don't want to lead the rest of my life alone, Judy."

Judy looked momentarily into her mother's beautiful, resentful eyes, and her own resentment flared up.

"Not at all. There's nothing criminal about it. It's just . . . very distasteful to both Pat and me to know that you are putting somebody in Daddy's shoes."

Katherine began to tremble, although she had reminded herself before this scene took place that she *must* keep calm, no matter what this foolish child did or said.

"You aren't at all kind, Judy. You make everything seem so very unattractive. I am not 'putting someone else in Daddy's shoes.' Nobody could ever take your father's place."

"That's what we think," muttered Judy darkly.

Katherine strove for patience.

"There's no need to bracket yourself with Pat. He is being decent enough to try and accept the situation even if it *is* distasteful to him."

Another shrug from Judy.

"He can do what he likes. I keep telling you it doesn't hit him as hard as it hits me."

Katherine thought:

43

"I must try to remember that all this is really because she loves me so much. I must try to feel flattered instead of angry towards her. Poor little Judy."

"Darling," she said gently. "I can't believe you mean to be so absolutely self-centered about this thing. Look . . . I know it has hit you and I assure you that I have refused Uncle Robert—Robert as he wants you to call him—a great many times on account of you two. I've given in because I love him, Judy. You're nearly twenty. Surely you understand a bit about human nature, and can make allowances for my getting fond of another man—even though it isn't the same way in which I was fond of your father. He will always have his own niche. My love for Robert Tracy is quite different. And to show you how far he respects the memory of your father, he offered to do quite a wonderful thing, which I'll tell you about. When I told him that I could hardly bring myself to take off the wedding-ring which hasn't been off my finger since your father died . . . he said he quite understood and that he would take it and have the gold fused into his own so that the two rings become one, and I would be wearing both. Could any man have thought of anything more charming? It shows you what terribly nice ideas he has."

Silence. A large bumble bee hummed through the open casement, circled around the kitchen table and settled on the edge of the honeypot which lay on the deal table between mother and daughter. Vaguely the girl watched it. She was forced, secretly, to agree that that was a charming idea of Robert's but it did nothing to lessen her antipathy for him or her distaste for the whole idea of passionate love between him and her mother.

"Oh, I don't know!" at length she cried. "Perhaps it's because I'd always felt that you were *ours*, Pat's and mine, and that we would always have you and our own home. That's why I can't bear the idea of your breaking it all up."

Tears filled Katherine's eyes. She did not cry easily, but she was emotionally worn out and she had slept so badly last night, tossing and turning, worrying about Judy. She put a hand out and laid it on the girl's arm.

"Darling, you know how much I adore you and Pat—and our little cottage. I still do. I always will. My marrying

Robert won't ever alter that. It will merely mean a move to Cooltye Farm, and I shall have someone to look after me when I'm older. *You'll* marry in time, Judy, you know it. You won't think twice of leaving me then."

"That's natural."

Katherine forced back her tears and gave a wry smile.

"Is it so unnatural for a woman of forty-one to want to get married?"

"I suppose to me it is . . . anyhow, that's how I feel about it. I admit I'm being self-centered, but it's broken up my home and I don't see eye to eye with my future stepfather. So it's better for me to quit."

Katherine stared at the girl. She was amazed to think how implacable one so young could be. Yet reminded herself that youth is always so . . . far less tolerant than age. A few years more and Judy would have understood this thing and accepted it with a so much better grace. Deep depression filled the mother's soul. In a low tone she said:

"So you mean to leave me when I need you most?"

Judy's head shot up.

"You don't need *me,* you've got *him!*"

"No husband can take your place. You are my daughter," said Katherine gently.

"What should you want me for . . . just to sit and play gooseberry while you two hold hands on the sofa?"

Katherine went scarlet and rose to her feet.

Quickly Judy apologized:

"Oh, I'm sorry. That was unpleasant of me."

"Very," agreed her mother stiffly.

"Well—surely you can see!" Judy sought to justify herself. "It will mean a threesome from now onwards, so why should I like it? He won't want me hanging around, even if you do."

"Oh, Judy!" exclaimed her mother in a voice of despair. "You are so determined to hate Robert!"

"Not at all. I tell you I feel *dead,* indifferent, to him. I used to feel resentful because he ticked me off, but perhaps he always guessed he was going to be my stepfather, and played the part in advance."

Katherine shook her head. She was speechless. There

seemed no way of breaking through the crust of Judy's disproportionate jealousy. But it was the old childish Judy who added:

"The only decent thing he ever did was to give me my dog, Titus. I adored *him*. But I think I'm rather glad poor Titus died when he did. I don't want to be under any obligation at any time to *him*."

Katherine swung round on her.

"Your attitude towards Robert is absolutely mean and unreasonable."

Judy gave a bitter smile.

"There you are! That's what would always be happening if I stayed here. He would always come between you and me. That's why I'm going away."

"Oh, darling, won't you give us a chance!" cried Katherine, anguished.

Judy's gaze softened a little as she saw the pain on her mother's loved face. She could willingly have broken down now and wept; said that she would accept the whole situation and stay . . . the last thing she wanted to do was to leave Cooltye and the Dower House and her country home. But she was nothing if not logical and clearsighted. She knew that she would come to blows with Robert Tracy in the future if not at once . . . even if she could bring herself to live under his roof and call the farm her "home." Even if she could bear to see him treating Mummy as his wife . . . particularly in the honeymoon stage, she thought distastefully. Judy, too, had had a bad night, and thought about things for hours on end. And she had reached the definite conclusion that she would be better in London working for Elizabeth. Besides, she felt that there was not a vestige of the child left within her. It had made her more conscious of Tony . . . of wanting Tony to cherish and comfort her.

Yet she did not like to see that look of misery in the eyes of the mother whom, in her heart of hearts, she still most deeply loved.

She went forward and put her arms round the slight figure and kissed Katherine on the cheek.

"Sorry, Mummy, if I'm being a brute. But I *can't* pretend. You know I've never been a hypocrite. I dare say Pat's a much nicer character, and you and your . . . Robert . . . will be much more pleased with him than with me . . . but I can't *pretend* to like what's happened, nor can I bring myself to live at the Farm. Please try to understand."

She released her mother before the older woman had the chance to return the embrace, and walked quickly to the kithchen door.

Desperately Katherine called after her:

"Judy, don't go like that. . . . Let's go on talking. . . ."

"Mummy, I *can't*," said Judy with tight lips and crimson cheeks. "There's nothing more to discuss and it only upsets us both. I'm going up to town with Pat on Tuesday. I'm sorry, but there it is."

Katherine Green stood rigid, every nerve in her body quivering with pain and resentment.

She knew that she could have said a lot of silly things about Judy still being under age and all that . . . trying to force her to remain here . . . or even bursting into tears and *imploring* her to remain, trying to appeal to the softness which she knew was really there under the girl's harsh exterior.

But there was a certain strength of character and pride in Katherine's own character which would not allow her to make a sentimental appeal of that kind. If this was what Judy had chosen—so be it. But nothing would induce her to believe that Judy really meant to go.

5

But Katherine was forced to realize that Judy was a creature of her word. When that Tuesday morning came she was fully packed and dressed, ready to leave Cooltye with her brother.

Nobody could say that it had been a happy weekend. There had been very few ruffles on the surface, but underneath all three of them had been badly disturbed and fraught with anxiety for the future.

Sunday night had been the most wretched Katherine could remember . . . for usually they were so jolly, with Robert coming over for cold supper and all of them playing rummy or listening to a radio play. And sometimes their friends, the Haddons, dropped in for coffee and spent the evening with them. Katherine was a great favourite in the village, particularly with the children, who loved her and read her books. Bill Haddon, the local physician—a man of about Katherine's own age—as his own wife put it, "thought Katherine the cat's whiskers." Joyce herself was fifteen years younger than the doctor—a sports-loving, capable, happy-go-lucky sort of girl, who already had two babies to look after. Joyce Haddon shared her husband's admiration for Katherine, and was a frequent visitor at the little cottage. Many had been the times when Joyce lost her domestic help and Katherine, after a morning's writing, would walk across the fields to the Haddons' house and take the babies out for a walk while Joyce attended to the cooking.

On this particular Sunday evening the Haddons did not come in for coffee because they had Joyce's mother and father staying with them. So it had been a difficult foursome. Robert had made an obvious effort to be cheerful and friendly, and behave as though nothing had happened, and even Judy could not accuse him of paying any marked attention to her mother in public. He studiously avoided doing so, and only the odd "Kath darling" dropped from his lips.

Katherine, in her turn, tried to be natural. Pat, unhappy in his mind (more particularly because he was aware of his sister's attitude), covered his feelings by making more of a noise than usual, trying to get foreign stations on the wireless. Judy was icily polite to Robert and quite unnaturally so with her mother, and excused herself as soon as the washing up was done by saying that she had a headache and was off to bed.

Once she was alone with Robert, Katherine had relaxed for a moment, surrendered hungrily to his quick, passionate embrace, and then shut her eyes and shook her head despairingly.

"Oh, Rob, what a time I've had! They hate it so. And Judy *is* going. She gave in her notice at the Dower House yesterday. She has packed everything in her room. It breaks my heart."

Robert had pulled a pipe from his pocket and stuck it in the corner of his mouth, his heavy brows drawn together. The kindly, intelligent eyes which had first drawn her to him rested upon her face with a touch of sadness.

"I feel horribly to blame for all this, my poor Kath. At the same time nothing will induce me to throw in my hand and offer to release you. I *know* inside myself that this is only a temporary setback. Young Judy will come round. Just leave her alone. You'll see. She's far too fond of you to let such a state of affairs continue."

Katherine swallowed hard. She went to the mirror, which hung against one of the beams, and stared at herself. She looked tired and angular tonight, she thought, and every inch a woman of forty. All her radiance (loving and being loved by Robert had made her feel a girl again) was dimmed by this battle with her young daughter.

She gave a long, deep sigh.

"I look a hag," she muttered.

Robert came up behind her and put an arm round her slender shoulders, smiling at her reflection in the mirror.

"You look very beautiful to me, darling, but you're tired. You're not sleeping well, are you?"

"Not a wink," she admitted with a half-laugh.

"Try not to let it get too much on your mind, sweet. Let the child go to town and learn from experience how foolish she has been," he begged her. "And don't worry about her. She has good friends, hasn't she?"

"Yes. This girl, Elizabeth Chapman, who runs the flower shop, is very nice, and has very nice people who live in town. And I like the son, Tony. He is the medical student whom Judy calls her 'boy friend.' But, oh, Rob, she's barely twenty. It will be her twentieth birthday in August. She's so very young. I did so want her to stay at home with me for a bit longer."

Robert had tried to comfort and counsel her. By the time he left she had felt better—strengthened spiritually as she always was after an hour or two with Robert. He was so wonderfully understanding. Some men might have been thoroughly "put off" by his reception from his future stepchildren, and resented it. He really was a lamb, her Rob, and the more she thought about it the greater grew her conviction that he was the right man for her to marry and that she would be mad to lose him just because Judy was being a little fool.

But it was an unhappy mother who saw her two children depart for London after breakfast that Tuesday morning. She had made no further appeal to Judy and the girl had disappointed her bitterly by not showing any sign of softening. Yet her heart was wrung even more by her son than the daughter who positively refused to live with her any more. Pat had tried to be friendly. Pat had wished her luck. But not once had she heard him shout with laughter as he used to do. As a family they always adored Pat's great guffaw of laughter when he was amused. He had been strangely silent: that had made Katherine fear he was miserable. He did not show his feelings like his sister, but Katherine was deeply concerned about him. Just before he went she hugged him and whispered in his ear:

"I'm sorry if I've upset you, my darling. I mean . . . do forgive me for getting married again. It won't make any difference between *us*. I promise it won't."

He reddened and twitched uncomfortably, but hugged her back.

"That's O.K., Mum. I'm all for the wedding and a spot of fizz, so let me know when it's to be. I expect I'll still be at Colchester. We're training there during the summer, and going into camp next month, but I'll wangle a 'forty-eight'."

Gratefully she kissed him. Then turned to Judy. Judy was very pale this morning, and looked a complete stranger to her mother. So very "London" in her best dark suit and with a little straw hat and veil. (Judy, who never wore a hat!) *And* those gloves. And two suitcases. Katherine's whole throat constricted. She wanted to throw her arms round that rigid young figure and beseech her to drop the cases and stay. But Judy gave her a tight little smile and said:

"Well, bye-bye, Mummy. I'll write to you and let you know my address. Elizabeth said on the 'phone that she thought she knew somewhere cheap for me, but I shall be staying with her tonight. Her people have asked me. In Draycott Avenue . . . near Peter Jones. I've left the address on your desk."

Pat moved away unhappily. Katherine bit hard on her lip in the effort not to cry.

Robert had told her to meet Judy's explacability with hardness on her own side, rather than allow the girl to think she could control her mother's life with such abominable selfishness. Robert was right, of course, but Katherine had never been more unhappy since her husband died than when she saw Judy walk away, carrying one case, and her brother beside her with the other.

So she meant it! And tonight she would sleep with the Chapmans and tomorrow go into "digs" all on her own. Judy . . . her little girl. . . .

Anger mingled with Katherine Green's heartbreak. She turned back into her cottage, followed by the two Corgis, and fiercely brushed away the stinging tears. Oh, the little idiot! To throw up her lovely home down here, in the middle of the summer, too, and all the chances of benefiting by a new home like Cooltye Farm, and with a man like Robert to take an interest in her. *Oh, the stubborn little egotist!*

Miserably, Katherine went up to her daughter's bedroom and looked at the emptiness of it.

Pat had said that he would come back for his next leave. Pat had promised to come to her wedding. But Judy, without saying so, had inferred that she would never come back. Indeed, on Saturday she had openly declared that she did not want to be asked to the wedding.

Katherine shut Judy's door behind her. Mrs. Askell from the village would be coming in to clean up later on. Tonight Katherine was going over to Cooltye Farm to dine and discuss plans for interior decoration. Robert wanted her to do up the drawing-room and her future bedroom to her own taste. He would deny her nothing within reason, she knew that; it would all be so much more comfortable there than here, this coming winter. He was even going to have central heating put into the farmhouse for her. It was a solid house, built in the days of Queen Anne, but could be very cold, as it stood high; but Robert had said he would make quite sure that she was warm and cosy when the north winds blew across the Downs from the sea. She was to decide, too, whether or not to pull out the present range and put in a new modern cooker. Oh, there would be many exciting, lovely things to talk about. And after the long years in this shabby, tiny place, following David's death, it meant much to Katherine to face a new full life as the wife of a man she could deeply love.

Yet it was all going to be ruined if it parted her from her children!

She lit a cigarette and, with the dogs tumbling after her, went down to the sitting-room and seated herself in front of her typewriter. She must finish another chapter if she was to get this book to the publishers before the autumn.

She looked blindly at the half-typed sheet in the roller. She kept seeing Judy's tight-lipped young face . . . horrified by the thought that Judy would not be coming back tonight, as usual, and that *she* would be quite alone. Cruel, cruel Judy to have gone off and left her like this. Cruel to punish her because she wanted to marry again.

Katherine's eyes, misting over with the ready tears again,

gazed out of the window, across the fields to Cooltye Farm. She set her teeth.

"But I'm going to marry you, Rob, I'm going to! I'm not going to let my own daughter or anybody else come between us now," she said aloud.

This decision was strengthened after seeing Joyce and Bill Haddon, later that day.

Katherine called in at Mulberry House for tea. It was a rather ugly stone residence, half covered with creeper, standing right in the centre of the village, facing the local garage. It had been the doctor's house as far back as anyone in Cooltye could remember. But it was comfortable enough inside and had had a new modern surgery built on to it.

Katherine, as soon as she arrived, told them rather nervously what had happened.

"I don't know what you think about my marrying Robert Tracy, but there it is . . . it's sort of been in the offing for some time now, only I've kept saying 'no' on account of Pat and Judy. Now I've said 'yes' and you see what's happened!"

The Haddons had listened to her attentively. The doctor, a big, nice-looking man with rather shaggy fair hair grizzling at the temples, and wearing horn-rimmed spectacles, stood in front of the fireplace with a cigarette between his lips and his hands in his pockets, his gaze fixed thoughtfully upon Katherine. (He had known David, her husband, and through the years he had watched the courageous struggle which Katherine had put up since her husband's death. In fact, Bill and David had taken their degree at the same hospital.)

Yet Bill had always hoped that Katherine would marry again. She was far too attractive to be "wasted." He had been half in love with her himself at one time, but that was ten years ago, and after David's death she had so obviously retired into a shell and devoted herself to her young family, and was not to be wooed or won. He had given up. Then, soon after Bill took over this practice, he had gone on a holiday to Austria, ski-ing. It was a sport to which he was devoted, and he had met young Joyce enjoying the same delights in the crisp snow, staying with her parents in the same hotel. Joyce, at twenty, had been very much what she was now . . . pretty, plump, utterly amiable, and great fun. He had fallen in love with her as an older man will with a very young girl who hero-worships him, and young Joyce, who had never cared much for boys of her own age, had immediately adored the big, shaggy-haired young doctor. Her parents liked him, and it was only a matter of a month or two before they were married. Bill found her a most cheerful and charming companion, who never grumbled no matter what domestic tragedies befell her or the children. In fact, she was the ideal wife for a country practitioner.

But he still had a corner in his heart for Katherine Green, and a very genuine interest in her welfare. Her news brought immediate and unhesitating approval from him.

"This is great, Katherine. What could be better? Don't you agree, Joyce? . . . Robert Tracy is a grand fellow and I think it's quite the best thing that could have happened."

Joyce, who never looked more than a schoolgirl even now, although she was twenty-six and had two babies, sat on the stool at Katherine's feet, hugged her knees, and fixed a pair of blue, glowing eyes on the older woman.

"Oh, what fun!" she exclaimed. "Congratulations, Katherine darling."

She just *adored* Katherine. She was so lovely, with her ash-blonde hair and fine-cut features, and those grave, lovely eyes. She had all the grace and beauty of movement, all the flair for dressing well and being gracious and charming, which Joyce felt that she, personally, lacked. And she had so often agreed with Bill that it was a shame that Katherine should remain a widow. Equally, the Haddons shared the opinion that she had spoiled her two children; they thought young Judy rather exacting, but liked her, and they were amused by Pat, and, of course, they could see that the two adored their mother. But neither Bill nor Joyce was surprised to hear that the news of Katherine's forthcoming marriage had not been well received by her two children. It was only to be expected when the three of them had been so close-knit and isolated together for so many years.

"Oh, but I think it's simply lovely!" Joyce added enthusiastically. "I'm so thrilled. Just think of you marrying Mr. Tracy. He's terribly nice, and the farmhouse is just *heaven*.

I always tell Bill it's my dream house, and I bet with your touches, Katherine, it will be *too* lovely."

Katherine drew in her breath. Their enthusiasm somehow supported her.

"Thanks, both of you!" she exclaimed. "I feel better now that I know you approve."

Bill kicked his toe gently against the fender.

"I presume the offspring have been difficult?"

"Well, as I have just told you, Judy has taken it very badly, but Pat's actually doing his best to be nice, the poppet."

"Judy's a selfish little brute," cried Joyce, quick in defence of her wonderful Katherine.

Dr. Haddon grimaced at her and affectionately tugged at a piece of her hair.

"You're only a child yourself and intolerant of other children. I can see how young Judy feels and it isn't altogether selfishness. It's a primitive reaction. How many young creatures like their mothers or fathers marrying again? Precious few."

Joyce looked up at him indignantly.

"But if she was really fond of Katherine, she'd be decent about it."

Katherine sighed and intervened on Judy's behalf.

"Bill's right; I see it, and even Robert does . . . Judy's point of view, I mean. I adored my own mother. Luckily for me she and my old Dad were together until they died. But I can imagine how I might have hated either of them giving me a 'step'!"

"So Judy's walked out," said Bill reflectively.

"Isn't it awful, Bill?" groaned Katherine.

"She'll be the loser. Fancy leaving *you* and Cooltye for 'digs' and a job in London," said Joyce.

"Come to think of it—rather plucky of her," said Bill. Joyce grimaced back at him.

"Always on the side of the young and pretty—my husband!"

"That's why I pursued you to the bitter end," he grinned.

"*Bitter end*, indeed!" Joyce pouted.

"Sweety-pie. . . ." He laughed and kissed the top of her head.

Katherine looked and listened, and thought:

"What a happy marriage theirs is! Mine will be, too, with Rob. I've missed this sort of comradeship all these years. I do owe it to myself to marry again. I must go on, in spite of Judy."

The doctor glanced at her and saw the unusual look of strain and anxiety on the beautiful face which had always seemed to him one of the most tranquil. Serenity—calm acceptance of sorrow—these things were part of Katherine Green's loveliness. He did not like to see her distress even though he tried to be just and to find excuses for her impetuous, possessive young daughter.

"Don't worry, Katherine," he said gently. "Judy will come round. She'll see which side her bread is buttered—amongst other things. It won't be easy for her fighting in London by herself."

"Oh, Bill! I didn't want her to *have* to fight. And that's why I feel so mean . . . as though I've walked over *her* to snatch at my own happiness."

"You are absolutely justified and it'll do her no harm. When the young have to fight their way in the world it makes for character. Doesn't do any good molly-coddling them. Life's too tough these days."

Katherine sighed and agreed.

Joyce jumped up and put an arm round her.

"I just can't bear you to be upset, but Bill's right. Judy will soon find out how foolish she's been. Now come upstairs and see your godchild."

"My pretty Kitty, She's so witty . . ." sang Bill lustily, but was interrupted by his wife.

"I won't have you calling our baby 'Kitty.' She's to be Katherine."

Upstairs with the adorable "Kitty," who was all eyes and golden curls at fifteen months old; and with the three-year-old Nicholas, who was exactly like Bill. Katherine regained some of her good spirit. She adored children and these two reminded her of her own at the same age. She was altogether feeling better by the time she reached Cooltye Farm.

It was Robert Tracy that evening who was depressed and in need of cheering. A stray dog, running wild, had killed two of this season's lambs. Robert had been out with his head man trying to trace the culprit, and had not yet washed and changed when Katherine reached the house. He apologized and bade her sit down and look at a book until he was ready.

All the maternal side in Katherine's nature came well to the fore as she put her arms round his neck and kissed him. She had never seen Robert's rather gaunt face look so gloomy.

"Never mind, darling, don't let it upset you too much. The poor lambs, though! And the poor old sheep. What we mothers go through is nobody's business."

"I oughtn't to touch you . . . I'm all hot and dusty," he murmured, but gratefully kissed the sweet mouth which was as fresh and fragrant as a girl's, and thrilled to the caress of one of her slim hands on his roughened hair.

"My adorable Kath," he added in a whisper.

"Hurry up and come down again. You look as though you need a drink and some food. I suppose you have been tramping the fields for hours."

He brushed away some of the grey dust from his corduroy breeches, and with a silk handkerchief wiped his brown neck and forehead.

"Yes . . . Armstrong and I covered quite a bit of land. But no sign of the damned dog. Fond though I am of animals, I'd like to . . . no, perhaps I wouldn't . . . I don't even like shooting a murderous mongrel."

"Dear Rob!"

"Pour yourself out some sherry, sweet," he said. "I won't be long."

She seated herself on a window seat by the windows, which were still open to the fading light of a long summer afternoon. She thought about this man she had promised to marry. His essential kindness. Robert couldn't hurt a fly. She was quite sure it wouldn't be him, but Armstrong, his head man, who would eventually fire at the "stray" if they ever found him chasing the sheep.

The door burst open and a large Collie bounded into the room. Robert's pet, Sally. She was a devoted slave to him and wonderfully trained. Robert had won several prizes with her in local sheep-dog trials lately. She came straight up to

Katherine, laid her head on her knee, and looked up at her with liquid golden eyes. Katherine fondled the smooth ears and thought of her two Corgis, whom Judy had christened Pip and Squeak, years ago, when they were puppies. Pip and Squeak would have to learn how to get on with Sally when they moved here, and Sally to accept them. More jealousies in the offing, she reflected ruefully. The Collie wouldn't much like two boisterous, barking Corgi dogs trespassing in her domain. Who else would object? Probably Mrs. Bunting, who had looked after Robert ever since he bought the Farm. An excellent woman, and the Buntings were well known in the village. Equally was it known that Mrs. Bunting preferred working "for gentlemen"—widowers or bachelors. She had a sharp tongue and didn't get on with the ladies. Katherine had never had anything to do with her, but could imagine she might object to a "mistress of the house"! However, Robert had talked about engaging a married couple, as he wanted another man on the farm, and the wife could do the cooking. And there was always Katherine's own Mrs. Askell for cleaning—a real old-type Sussex woman, who adored the whole Green family.

Dreamily, Katherine looked round. This was a long, well-proportioned room, with its mullioned window which overlooked a small flower garden, and glimpsed a fair-sized duck-pond and belt of trees beyond. The farm buildings, stables and garage, were at the back. There were some lovely beams in here, but the walls had been papered in Victorian style, and there were a lot of rather dull pictures which had at one time been given to Robert by a sister—now dead—along with a rather ugly cabinet full of china standing over there in the corner. The furniture was solid and good and there was an enormous bookcase full of books, which Katherine liked. Robert—like herself—was an insatiable reader.

But, as he had so often admitted to Katherine, the house, which could be beautiful, was furnished without taste and definitely dull. He was going to give her scope to alter it as she wished. He relied on her taste, and had always said how charming the little cottage was, due to her light artistic touch.

"My poor Rob needs a woman here to make it all bright
and gay and to look after him," she thought while she waited
for him to come downstairs again, and she amused herself
by redecorating and arranging this room in her mind's eye.
Apple green and rose pink chintzes to replace those awful
art-satin curtains which ruined the room. The carpet was a
fine green Wilton and could remain. The walls must be
stripped and either painted or repapered in cream. Away
with that ghastly chocolate paint on dado and picture rail.
Away with the pictures, too! Except that one nice Peter
Scott—herons flying over the marshes—a fine piece of
colour. She would bring all her own cushions and her Queen
Anne winged armchair which had belonged to David's grand-
father. Her collection of pewter for the dining-room, too,
and her frilled dressing-table and the adorable patchwork
quilt which had been made by her own grandmother and
lasted through the years. It would look lovely on the wonderful oak four-poster bed which was in the spare room
and which Robert had bought with the farmhouse. A real
Tudor piece. That room would become theirs because it had
heavenly windows facing east and west and got all the sun.
It looked across Robert's pasture land to the South Downs.

Her thoughts rambled on. The farmhouse was so full of
potentialities and Rob would like everything that she did.
They would enjoy it together.

She was going to be very, very happy. And it would be
wonderful when darling Pat came home here for leave. He
would come, she knew it. As for Judy . . . her mother's heart
surged with longing to placate her rebellious daughter.

"I'll write her first thing in the morning." She thought,
without resentment, of the pain and grief Judy had caused
her. "I'll tell her how much she means to me and beg her
again to give this all a chance."

In came Robert, newly shaven, bathed, looking, as he always did in the evenings, debonair in a well-cut grey suit.
The thin, bony face was smiling now and quite boyish and
eager as he hurried towards her.

"All set for that drink? Hope I haven't been too long,
darling?"

"Any time spent away from you is too long, Rob," she murmured.

"It's very wonderful for me to see you here and know that very soon you will be living under this roof . . . my very own," he said, taking her in his arms.

"Oh, I long for it, too!" she breathed, and rubbed her cheek against his shoulder.

He kissed her hair.

"As usual, you smell heavenly, Kath."

"I was about to say how nice *you* smell," she laughed. "A clean, soapy, smoky sort of scent."

He laughed and moved away from her.

"The authoress romancing . . . bless you, Kath! Well, I'll go and get that sherry bottle and then we'll talk. Mrs. B. is in the kitchen. She's condescended to serve up some supper."

"Have you told her . . . about us?"

"She knows," he grinned. "I think everybody in Cooltye guesses already without the announcement appearing in the paper, my love. Your young son told Baxter at the garage, and I think he must have passed the news on every time he filled up a local car with petrol."

Katherine bit her lip. She felt strangely excited and happy tonight, even with the shadow of Judy hovering a little menacingly in the background.

"What does Mrs. Bunting say?"

Robert pulled his nose and blinked.

"A little uppish. 'My *con*-gratulations, I'm shore!' she said when I saw her this morning. And looked like sour milk."

Katherine laughed.

"I don't suppose she'll stay."

"I couldn't care less, as the young say today," laughed Robert.

As he walked towards the dining-room Katherine called after him:

"Bill and Joyce Haddon approve, anyhow. They think it's a fine idea."

"They're good types," Robert called back.

He added as he returned with a bottle and two glasses:

"We can afford to laugh at the world, my Katherine. We

love each other, and want to live together, and that's the main thing. With your permission I shall see the Rev. Mr. Jenners tomorrow and have our banns read next Sunday. I don't see any object in waiting. Young Judy's careered off, and why should you live alone? How about fixing our Day for three weeks' time?"

She caught her breath, her eyes like stars dancing at him —her cheeks warm and pink. He thought as he looked at her that in this golden light of the summer evening she might have been the same age as her daughter. Silently he marvelled at her agelessness and the beauty that was promised to him.

"I didn't think of a wedding quite so soon, Rob!" she breathed.

He poured out the sherry.

"Any objection?"

Her long fine lashes flickered. She frowned and tried to think . . . to weigh it all up. She had told the children that she didn't expect to get married till the autumn. Yet Rob was right, why should she live alone? It would have been different had Judy still been with her; then she would have wanted to give the girl time to get accustomed to the change-over. But Judy had gone. Katherine's heart beat fast with the thrilling thought of spending the rest of the summer in this house with Robert. *Three weeks' time.* That meant the middle of July. All the rest of the lovely warm days here with *him*. No more "good nights" or "good-byes"—no more solitude.

She had that book to finish. Well, that wouldn't take her more than another fortnight if she worked hard, and without Judy to cook for there would be more time. She herself was content with a picnic. She usually went to such a lot of trouble to feed the children. (She must try to stop thinking of them as children. Pat was in the Army and Judy had gone up to London to earn her own living!)

Robert handed her a glass, smiling down at her flushed face.

"Am I rushing you, darling? It's just that I want you so much and seem to have waited so long."

She tried to be practical. There was this house to do up, and her own cottage to sell, her trousseau to buy. Couldn't possibly be done in so short a time, she protested.

Robert raised her glass and toasted her, "To my love." Then he began to argue gently that nothing need be done in a hurry. She could just move here and put the cottage up for sale. As for painting this place, there were ways and means . . . if she decided on the colour scheme he would get a chap he knew in Brighton to come over and do it all. A builder who was a pal and could soon put a coat of paint or some paper in the house. Besides, they would have a honeymoon—that would mean they would be away for a fortnight and much could be achieved in their absence. He hadn't taken two weeks off from this place since he started farming it. He needed a holiday, so did Katherine. Armstrong was quite capable of carrying on until he came back, and as long as he personally was here when they started cutting the corn and haymaking, it didn't matter. He had a first-rate lot of workers at the moment, and the place would run itself, really. Where would she like to go? He'd heard that Austria was the answer. . . . France and Italy were both very dear just now. But one of his friends had just come back from ten days in a Schloss on the edge of a lake in Austria, with the mountains behind it, and said that it was staggeringly beautiful, and that one's pound went a long way out there.

"Would you like me to write to this Schloss and fly you to Austria for your honeymoon, Kath?"

The tempo of Katherine's heartbeats increased. After so many years of widowhood—of leading a reserved, sequestered existence, alone with her children and few friends—the very thought of a honeymoon in a castle on an Austrian lake sounded wildly romantic—and improbable.

Yet if she wanted these delights—wanted to have this fine, strong, dependable man at her side as her husband—she could have them all, in three weeks' time.

"Oh, Rob!" she said, swallowing hard.

He put down his glass, took her hand and kissed it.

"It isn't just a piece of fiction, Kath. It can be made a reality if you'll just say the word, my love."

Into the background crept Judy's shadow and the memory of her heartbreaking cruelty and defiance. Just for the moment (although Katherine well knew that it was only for the moment) there was no place in her thoughts for either of her children. She grew suddenly reckless and almost mad with happiness. She went into Robert's arms like an eager girl.

"Oh, I'd adore it! I can think of nothing more wonderful. You shall put the banns up, Rob, and we'll get married just when you say. As for Austria . . . it's a place I've wanted to see all my life."

"I hope I shall be able to give you lots of things in your life that you've wanted and not had," he murmured, caressing her hair. "I love you very much, you know."

"And I love you," she whispered back. "I can feel in my bones tonight that we're going to be terribly happy in this house."

His kisses . . . the touch of his hands . . . the adoration in his eyes, and all the exciting plans they made that evening were almost like narcotics for Katherine. She gave herself up to it completely. It was only when she got home to her little cottage, and he had left her there, that reaction set in and she began to remember Judy and Pat again. To feel the unaccustomed loneliness . . . to miss the daughter who used always to be here to welcome her if they had not gone out together.

It *had* been a wonderful evening at Cooltye Farm, and she had come home feeling elated, as though she were walking on air. Yet suddenly the problem of Judy returned in full force, and with it the memory of those words: *"Don't ask me to come to the wedding!"*

Katherine walked to her bureau and picked up a photograph which had been done of Judy about a year ago. So like her still, only a smiling Judy who looked at her with fond gaze. She whispered to the pictured face:

"Oh, but you *will* come to my wedding . . . you mustn't spoil things for me now. I'll *make* you change your mind, Judy, my darling."

But the cold finger of doubt touched Katherine's heart even as she said the words.

6

ABOUT two weeks later Judy Green shook the raindrops from her umbrella and took off her nylon waterproof and beret in the florist's shop known as *Fleurette*. She was alone in the place this morning. Elizabeth Chapman was in bed with a sore throat. Judy felt rather important. She was to manage the shop "all on her own." But she felt far from cheerful. The weather was appalling; had changed overnight from the warmth of golden June to a damp cold which would have been more seasonable in winter. The little shop struck chilly and looked grey and dark. Hastily Judy switched on the fluorescent lighting, pulled back the curtains and stood for a moment looking at the flowers which had not been sold yesterday.

There was plenty to do. *Fleurette* was only a tiny place in a narrow street just off the Brompton Road, but Elizabeth had made an instant success of it. Her prices were reasonable and she offered small, pretty, made-up bunches, ready to put in bowls or vases, at a fixed price according to size. This had been popular with busy housewives. She also had the regular job of supplying flowers to a local restaurant.

She was making enough profit now to be able to give Judy a salary of five pounds a week, which she hoped to raise in time. They had planned to find a larger shop and increase business next summer.

So far as the work went—Judy found it fascinating. Elizabeth, professionally trained, had shown her how to decorate the window, arrange flowers and greenery to best advantage, make up sprays and buttonholes quickly, or larger bouquets for more important gatherings. She had taken to the job, as Elizabeth put it, like a "duck to water," and looked fresh and engaging in the pale rose overall which she wore in the shop. She had already gathered a little clientele of her own—apart from Elizabeth's. One business man who lived close by dropped in every afternoon, late, on his way home from the City, to buy flowers from Judy for his invalid wife. Elizabeth teased her about her "old boy friend," and said she was sure he liked looking at Judy's glowing young face as much as at the flowers.

Oh, it was a good job—a rewarding one—and in pleasant surroundings. And Judy was nearly always too busy to think. Today, alone here, she would be "hectic," she reflected, once the fresh-cut flowers arrived in their long boxes from Covent Garden.

Yet she found herself quite often remembering—and missing—her old job in the Dower House among the antiques. And more than that—missing the Thatched Cottage and Mummy. Not that she would dream of admitting it, even to her dearest friend. No—not even to Tony, who was growing more than ordinarily dear. (And she was willing to admit that!) But miss Mummy and home she did. And she felt guilty of having hurt her mother. But she remained adamant about it all. She could not and would not retract her decision to boycott Robert Tracy and his home, once her mother married him.

The Chapman family had been very kind to Judy. She had seen a lot of them; stayed as their guest for three days when she first left Cooltye, and dropped in most evenings now (Tony saw to that! If Tony was too busy with his medical studies to take her out). The Chapmans had a pleasant, largish maisonette in Draycott Avenue, and Elizabeth, by a stroke of luck, had found Judy a room only three doors away from them, where she paid thirty-five shillings a week, including breakfast.

As Judy opened up the shop and slipped into her pink overall her mind wandered to that "bed-sitting-room" which was now her "home." How she hated it, on her first night there! Cramped, dreary, with ugly blue paint and washed-out curtains, a threadbare carpet and divan bed. Just a chest of drawers with mirror on it, a painted deal cupboard for her clothes (one of those atrocities that nearly fell on top of you every time you tried to open the door). A gas fire and ring (shilling in the metre). A depressing outlook on sooty backyards and chimneys. It was a back room. That was why it was cheap, as the neighbourhood was good. And it was highly "respectable" because Mrs. Chapman had gone into all that on behalf of her daughter's young friend before Judy went there. Mrs. Purdy, who owned the place and let rooms, was like her dwelling—shabby, dreary, but integral, and did her best in the face of heavy odds. There were so many stairs to climb and to clean, and a succession of maids, both English and foreign, came and went . . . mostly went. Mrs. Purdy did the breakfasts. That first meal had depressed Judy after the lovely wholesome ones Mummy used to give her in their pretty kitchen at home. Tough cold toast, weak tea, bluish milk (oh, where was the thick creamy milk from the hated Uncle Robert's farm?). A cereal one day, fish the next, and occasionally a shop egg, which Judy despised. She began to realize how spoiled she had always been at home. She didn't much like being alone in that ugly "bed-sit," either. But this, she told herself, was the price of her liberty and her pride. She had announced to Mummy and Pat that she meant to earn her own living and look after herself rather than accept Robert Tracy as a stepfather. Nothing should defeat her.

So far she had not "suffered" very much. The lonely, shabby room and unappetizing breakfasts were pin-pricks, really. And she spent all day in the lovely flower shop with Elizabeth and often went out at night to eat with darling Tony. As for lunch—a "snack" at some local tea shop sufficed.

But it was something of a strain after her normal easy routine at Cooltye. And more than anything Judy missed the country. London was horrible in the summer. She felt suffocated—especially at weekends. Sunday was the worst day. So boring. Nothing to do. And she *could* have gone down to Cooltye to the cottage. Mummy had written several times (such gentle, unaccusing letters) begging her to relent and go back. But Judy answered that she "couldn't get away." *She would not go* and have to accept Robert Tracy as Mummy's promised husband.

Judy could not even have the pleasure of seeing her brother at the moment. Pat had gone into camp and was getting no leave until August. He had never been much of a correspondent, so she had received only one brief note since they left home, telling her where he was and asking how "Snub Nose" was getting on as a flower-girl!

She wrote back with forced enthusiasm, telling him life was wonderful. She wasn't going to admit to brother Pat that she felt desperately home-sick and frequently inclined to chuck pride to the winds and rush down to the cottage and Mummy again.

Tony, of course, bolstered up her morale whenever they were together. He was delighted that she had come to live in town, where he could see a lot of her. And he staunchly upheld her conduct. He was as intolerant as she herself.

"If my poor Papa perished and Mamma announced that she was replacing him—I'd be off like a shot out of a pop-gun," had been his comment when she first explained the situation.

Mrs. Chapman was equally sympathetic. She was older than Katherine Green and a completely different type. Her husband was an insurance broker, and they had been moderately well off, although the war had crippled them and Mr. Chapman's health had necessitated retirement, so that they had a fair struggle these days to keep the big maisonette going and maintain their old standards. Elizabeth had been to the best school—then they had paid for her Constance Spry training. Tony had been to Shrewsbury and was still a liability until he was qualified. And Mrs. Chapman liked social life . . . was smart and as slim as Judy's mother . . . and handsome (Tony had inherited her dark, fine eyes) . . . but in a hard way, and she used a lot of make-up, and her hair had not been allowed to go grey. She liked expensive clothes and played a lot of bridge. In her fashion she was a good wife and devoted mother. But it often seemed to Judy when she was with the Chapman family that Enid Chapman could never have made the sacrifices for Elizabeth or Tony that her own mother had made for her and Pat, nor worked so hard at a typewriter and in the kitchen. Enid was the type who always managed to get somebody to work for her. Even now she had a German cook-general who left her free to potter round the shops or go to her bridge club every day.

By comparison with Mummy, Judy fully realized, Enid Chapman fell very far short of that industrious and lovable woman down in Cooltye. And the knowledge irked Judy's spirit and made her conscience squirm. Yet she drank in, thirstily, the words with which Mrs. Chapman had upheld Judy when she first came to town.

"I think you have done the right thing and shown a lot of pluck, my dear. I'm so glad our Liza is able to give you a job with prospects. Far be it from me to critize your very nice mother, but I know were I left a widow I could *never* marry again. I might *want* to, but I wouldn't, because Tony and Liza would dislike it so."

This speech had mollified Judy, and sounded very noble. Though at times when she entered the Chapman household and saw Enid Chapman, heavily made up and dressed in the *"dernier cri,"* rushing off to her bridge, she wondered how long such noble sentiments would endure if Mrs. Chapman ever indeed found herself widowed.

But for the moment Judy was content to allow herself to be carried along on the tide of encouragement which the whole Chapman family poured over her. And she did not return to Cooltye.

It seemed the "end" when Mummy announced that she was getting married to Uncle Robert on July 15th (quite forgetting how long both Katherine and Robert had waited), and she was still more wretched when she had a note from her old friend and employer from the Dower House, informing her that everyone in the village had been "full of curiosity and surprise" when they heard the banns read out by Mr. Jenners at Cooltye Church.

"You could have knocked us all down with a feather," wrote Miss Tomlinson, Judy's former employer who ran the teashop in the Dower House. *"Of course we knew Mr. Tracy was very friendly with your mother, but none of us expected a romance. Of course I knew your dear father and can remember the awful days after he died, when your little mother used to say her heart was broken. Isn't it amazing how time*

*can soften these blows? I expect you are rather upset and that
is why you left home so suddenly, although you didn't really
tell me at the time. Poor child, I am sorry for you, but of
course your mother has every right to marry again if she
wants to. But I know how you must feel, because I feel the
same, after years of friendship with dear Dr. Green. . . ."*

The letter rambled on—sympathetic on the surface but
with just a catty layer underneath which made Judy writhe.
She exaggerated its importance and, forgetting that Miss
Tomlinson—although a just and God-fearing woman—was
herself a disappointed spinster, obviously jealous of the success of a more attractive woman of her own age, allowed it
to rankle. To fester in a mind already distorted on the subject until Judy pictured the whole village of Cooltye whisper-
ing about her mother and Robert Tracy . . . muttering
"poor Dr. Green."

When the final letter came from her mother begging her
to come down to the wedding, Judy wrote back a refusal.

She wrote it with foolish inconsistency—the tears pouring
down her cheeks, and her slim body shaken with sobs. A
silly, stilted little letter trying to pretend that she couldn't be
there because of work.

*"So terribly sorry, Mummy, but Elizabeth will be away
that day and there will be nobody in the shop but me. . . ."*

She was remembering that letter this morning while she
did her job. Lifting the glorious roses on their stiff long
stems with their half-opened buds, arranging them in tall
show glasses for the window, she kept seeing the other kind
of roses down at Cooltye. The good, old-fashioned country
flowers that Mummy loved. "Green is my name and green
are my fingers," Katherine used to laugh because everything
she planted came up and flourished.

Judy so much preferred those fat, dewy, *different* kind of
roses to this hot-house kind with their proud, unbending
necks. And she kept imagining, guiltily, the impression her
letter of refusal would have on Mummy when she read it.

At lunch-time Judy pulled down the blinds and locked

up *Fleurette* for an hour. (She had sold a lot of flowers: people needed cheering up this wet, unseasonable weather.) She was thankful that Tony was meeting her for lunch. She hadn't seen him or the family last night because she had gone to supper and a cinema with an old school friend who happened to be passing through London. Tony was to have a busy morning of lectures, but had promised to nip down to the Brompton Road at one o'clock to eat with her.

The moment they were at the table in the small restaurant, and after ordering their meal, he looked at her critically. He could see that all the sparkle had gone out of Judy's eyes. She looked positively dejected today, and that was unlike Judy, who had such a sense of humour and liked to giggle with him about things. He said:

"What's up with you, Ju? Weather getting you down?"

She shook her head and said it was nothing to do with the weather.

"The old business . . . Mamma marrying again?" he suggested.

A brief nod from Judy and a tightening of her fresh red lips.

Tony Chapman lit a cigarette. He was a little older than Judy—her senior by four years. He was, of course, much older and more experienced in most ways and already in the fifth year of his training at Bart's. She was his first real "girl friend." He had, of course, had "fun and games," as he put it, with the odd nurse, and once thought himself in love with a woman older than himself—an affair which had rapidly been squashed by his family. He was a handsome boy and an intelligent one. Most girls threw him a sidelong glance, attracted by his merry, sloe-dark eyes which were almond-shaped and set a little slantingly in a thin chiselled face. Those eyes, a brownish skin and a thick mop of dark hair had been bequeathed to him by an Italian grandmother on his father's side. He was often teased about his "Neapolitan" appearance, and goodnaturedly accepted it—although nobody could have been more English in their upbringing or ideas than Tony.

He was a steady worker and deeply interested in his forthcoming career as a doctor. He knew that it was advisable that he should not contemplate marriage until he was fully qualified . . . although he had done his two years in the Services. . . . Until he started to see a lot of his sister's friend, Judy, the idea of matrimony had been far from his mind.

But since Judy had run away from home and joined Liza at *Fleurette* the idea had seeped into his consciousness more than once. He was rapidly falling in love with Judy. Only when he first left College had he pinned up photographs of Rita Hayworth or Betty Grable in his room and worshipped at the shrine of "Hollywood Glamour." Now he was older and more sensible, his fancy turning to just such a girl as this one. She was very young, of course, and in his estimation rather more innocent and less sophisticated than the average modern girl of her age, but that he found to her credit. He adored the white-hot fervour of Judy's youth. He admired her courage and the fact that she had the courage of her convictions. She didn't think it the right thing for her mother to re-marry, and she didn't like the man she was marrying, so Judy had forsaken all the comforts offered as bait and had come up here to an uncomfortable "bed-sit" to earn her own living. What could be more admirable? It would have been so much easier for her to accept the marriage against her principles, and enjoy what the seemingly well-off stepfather could offer.

Tony had discussed the whole thing time and time again with Judy. He knew that she felt it rather badly that her adored brother had, as she put it, "caved-in" and was ready to go down there and stand by his mother. But of course Tony saw Pat's side of it. It was different for a chap who was in the Army and away from home. It was poor little Ju who naturally felt it. Tony had in his own impetuous fashion decided that he would have walked out of the house if Mamma had "put a bloke in Pop's shoes." So he upheld Judy's action even though he had a secret admiration for Katherine Green. During the off weekends he had spent down at the cottage he had always thought her a most beautiful and attractive woman for her age.

He had also met Robert Tracy and neither liked nor disliked him. But a gentleman farmer had nothing in common with Tony, whose hobbies outside medicine were music and the ballet. Judy loved the ballet, too, and they stood patiently in queues in all weathers to watch Margot Fonteyn and Robert Helpmann.

In fact, Tony and Judy had many tastes in common, and he was immensely thrilled, too, by her physical beauty. There was something so gloriously healthy and fragrant about Judy Green. Those brilliant grey-blue eyes . . . the burnished curly hair . . . the skin that glowed with health—golden, now, with a summer tan that needed no cosmetics. One or two of his friends at the hospital admired her enormously. Tony had reached the jealous stage, and that, undoubtedly, was the first sign of real love.

He tried to cheer her up during their cheap and simple lunch, but he could see that her thoughts were only half with him today. Finally he stopped trying and gave her a serious and compassionate look.

"You're in a bad way this morning, Ju. But you mustn't let it get you down. It doesn't do to be too rigid, you know, and it might make things easier for you, as you've got such a conscience and soft heart, if you *went* to this wedding."

Judy's curly head shot up.

"And let Robert Tracy think I'm climbing down? And shake hands and say 'God bless the bride'? Oh no . . . nothing doing!"

Tony grinned.

"Well, you needn't go as far as that. You can ignore the bridegroom. But you're really very fond of your mother, and she *is* rather a poppet, isn't she? You don't want to hurt her too much."

Judy chewed fiercely at her lips—her brow stormy, her big eyes searching for an answer to her problems which was not to be found.

"That's the trouble. It's all so difficult because Mummy's so sweet. Sometimes I feel I oughtn't to begrudge her her happiness, if she really wants this, and I *can't* get over it; after all this time, putting someone in Daddy's place and choosing Uncle Robert."

"You've got yourself all worked up, and anti-Uncle Robert, haven't you, sweety?"

"I dare say. But he doesn't like *me*, either. I'll never forget the way he ticked me off in front of my mother, and I dare say he'd start ticking me off, even at my age, if I consented to live at the Farm."

"There I'm fully in sympathy with you. But if I were you I'd nip down to the wedding so as not to rouse too much comment in the village. You don't want to snub your mother too publicly."

Judy's cheeks flamed.

"I believe you're on *her* side. . . ."

Tony put a hand under the table and laid it on her knee, with a gesture which suddenly thrilled her out of her despondency.

"Judy, darling, don't be a little idiot. You know whose side I'm on. I was only trying to help. I don't want you to do anything that you'll regret."

"I simply couldn't bear that wedding!" she said through her teeth, and found herself trying to remember the train service and wondering what train she could catch which would get her to Cooltye Church in time *if* she decided to go. IF . . .

"Oh, don't let's talk about it any more. I'm so fed up with it!" she exclaimed.

"I know you are, and I don't suppose it makes things any better for you to have to live all alone in that frightful 'bedsit.' I told Mamma and Liza the other night you ought to come and live with us."

"I couldn't possibly. But you're very sweet to me—all of you."

Now her hand stole into his under that little table. She felt his strong thin fingers catching hers in a grip that hurt. But she liked it, and her heart began to beat faster. She saw the look in his eye . . . a very new look . . . passionate and possessive.

"I suppose you realize I'm crazy about you, Judy?" he suddenly said in a low voice.

She hadn't realized it at all—although she had been crazy about *him* for some time. Happiness suddenly boiled up inside her and drove away all thoughts of Mummy's distasteful wedding. She caught her breath.

"Oh, Tony darling!"

"I knew it the other evening after we went to that film at the Polytechnic. I knew I didn't want to leave you outside Mrs. Purdy's horrible house. I wanted to take you home with me. No, not to Mamma's flat, but to a little home of our own. In other words, I wish to blazes we were married. Then you wouldn't mind so much about this marriage. You'd be too busy with your own!"

He ended with a slightly nervous laugh. It was rather nerve-racking, making serious love like this to a girl in a tiny restaurant which was crowded with other people, and quite against all his previous convictions that no medical student ought to get married. But Judy had looked so unhappy, Tony felt suddenly madly anxious to cherish and protect her.

"Don't you agree that it would be pretty marvelous if we could set up on our own?" he continued recklessly. "You could go on working with Liza and I would carry on with my training."

Judy gasped.

"Tony!"

Her heartbeats were shaking her whole body now. She had never been more agreeably surprised or thrilled. She was quite positive that she would like to get married to Tony Chapman, but she couldn't believe that it would be popular with his people—even though she *was* Liza's dearest friend. Tony was telling her now that he had a bit of money of his own—a legacy from an old aunt who had died about a year ago and left him about five pounds a week for life. Not much, but coupled with her salary and the allowance Pop gave him they could easily live in a cheap room somewhere together, and manage. And it would be a darned sight better than living apart—especially for Judy, who was all alone, he declared.

However, he didn't want to rush her, and as the whole thing wanted serious thought he ended the diatribe. And they mustn't do anything, anyhow, until he had taken his next exam at the end of the summer. Then—if he passed— he would feel they could go ahead and nobody at home would mind. They adored Judy; they would be glad he had made such a sensible choice.

"We could be engaged and have that to look forward to anyhow, sweety," he said.

Judy gave him a deep look from a pair of very brilliant eyes.

"Oh, Tony darling, I'm absolutely *staggered.*"

"And pleased?"

One dark, fine eyebrow went up in the way that Tony had. She loved those expressive brows. And that new intense look in his dark eyes made her feel dizzy with happiness.

"Oh, Tony, you know I've never thought about any man in the world except *you*," she said breathlessly.

"Darling, I wish we were alone so that I could kiss you," he whispered.

"I wish it, too," she whispered back rapturously.

And after a few minutes of saying all the lovely, absurd things to each other which young lovers have said from time immemorial, they came down to earth again. There was a cautious streak in Tony—a practical one—which made him say:

"Better not tell anybody until we've discussed it further, darling, and got things taped. We'll have the lounge to ourselves after supper. The parents have a bridge date and old Liza's in bed."

Judy nodded, gaze fixed upon him adoringly. Nothing seemed to matter now that she knew he loved her and that one day—perhaps *soon*—they would get married.

Then her face paled with sudden apprehension.

"Oh, Tony!" she said breathlessly. "I'm still under age! This stupid business about having to get parents' permission to marry. *Supposing Mummy disapproves?*"

Tony sat back, lit a cigarette and frowned.

"Oh, lord! Hadn't thought of that!" he said.

Now they sat gazing into each other's eyes anxiously. They had another problem to solve.

7

It was the morning of Katherine Green's wedding to Robert Tracy. With the help of the faithful Mrs. Askell, twenty-four hours ago, Katherine had packed up and closed down her little cottage.

Last night she had spent at Mulberry House with her good friends the Haddons.

She was going to be married from Mulberry House. It was Bill's and Joyce's wish. A friend was minding the two babies for Joyce, who wanted to hold a very small party here after the ceremony. She was going to be matron of honour and Bill was to give Katherine away.

"As an old friend of the family, I feel it my privilege," he had said when they talked things over.

When Katherine woke up in the Haddons' spare room that fateful day she felt in a complete daze. Happiness—the sweet excitement of the thought that this was good-bye to widowhood, and that in a few hours' time she would be Robert's wife—ran a swift race with doubt and apprehension. That tiny niggling doubt as to whether she ought to be doing this—because of Judy and Pat. *Only because of them.* She could not love Robert more. Her feeling for him had increased during these few weeks of their brief engagement. The faithful friend had become a devoted and attractive lover. And she was sure that he would make an equally perfect husband. Everything seemed so full of promise. The Brighton builder who was Robert's friend had done them proud, and Cooltye Farm was already freshly papered and painted. The new covers and curtains would be put up while they were abroad. The new home would be ready and waiting for them when they returned from their honeymoon.

76

Honeymoon! Katherine slipped out of bed, put on her dressing-gown and looked at the two suitcases—big Airways ones, both open—ready packed, waiting for the final odds and ends. Labelled *"Mrs. Robert Tracy"* with an address in Austria. Could anything be more exciting, or glamorous? They were flying to Paris this afternoon, then on to Strasbourg.

Katherine's pulses thrilled. Her mirror gave back the reflection of a slim woman with newly washed ash-blonde hair that looked like silver, with a crisp wave in it. A woman in her forties who might be ten years younger, with those eager, beautiful eyes of a girl, and only the faintest lines etched by time on an otherwise exquisite skin.

She *felt* like a girl again. Yet the memory of her two children persisted in giving her that unfortunate sensation of guilt—as though she had no right to feel so young or so gay. Unkind, implacable Judy! Refusing to come down to this wedding and so dimming the radiance for her mother, thought Katherine sadly. Yet she could not believe that in the end Judy would not be there. Only last night she had said to the Haddons: "I bet Judy will turn up. She won't want to hurt me so. . . ."

Dear old Pat was coming, bless him! He had even sent a wedding present. Hard up though he was, he had found a trifle to please her. A pigskin notecase with her new initials stamped on it. And he was coming on forty-eight-hours' leave, arriving in Cooltye in time for the wedding. Tomorrow he was spending with his sister in town.

An old friend of Robert's who was in the Navy, and with whom he had served during the war, was to be Robert's best man. Paymaster Lt.-Cmdr. Michael Cairn. A big, bluff, amusing fellow whom Katherine had met once or twice before and always liked. He was a confirmed bachelor, although Robert had said on the 'phone last night to her:

"Old Mike's full of envy. He says he wants to find himself a wife. He says if you make as fascinating a change in me as you've done in the house I'll have Hollywood after me, in spite of my nose."

Katherine had laughed back:

"I love your nose. And I should hate to make any change in you, my darling. I like you just as you are."

77

But she had been pleased, of course, at Michael's flattery. She thought of her children's book, finished, typed, and sent to the publisher. Of years of hard labour on that old Underwood . . . hours of planning to turn one pound into two and give Pat and Judy everything they wanted. Of cooking, housework and gardening.

Where was that sober-minded, routine-loving woman and mother? Bewitched, she seemed to have changed into this youthful, sparkling girl! Katherine looked at her wedding dress, which was hanging outside the cupboard. Navy-blue tie silk, with white organdie at the throat. A big white "cartwheel" hat with tiny feather-fronds round the brim. (It had come from Paris, and the price had made her feel hopelessly extravagant.) Then there was the well-cut dark blue coat in which she was going to travel. White gloves and bag lay on the dressing-table. Sheer nylons—Michael Cairn had brought three pairs of them back from Hong Kong and given them to her; new silky lingerie. She had tried the *ensemble* on last night, and Joyce and Bill had said she had looked "like a Vogue picture."

In the lapel of her coat she was wearing the diamond and sapphire star which David had given her. And that blue fox cape which looked so rich and silky and magnificent was Robert's wedding present—amongst many others!

Good-bye, indeed, if only for today, to the hard-working Katherine in her garden clothes. And it was enormous fun for once to be so fashionable, and to know that Robert would be dazzled and satisfied with his bride. And singular relief for her to sink into the luxury of being cared for and spoiled . . . to allow Robert to think of everything *for her*, in the way that David used to do. She had had so long of being the one to make the decisions. The children had been darlings, but much too young to help or advise.

How strange she had felt for the last week without her wedding-ring! There was a tiny white circle on the flesh of that slim, sun-burned finger. Soon her new wedding-ring—fused with the old—would be covering that white circle again.

It was funny, Katherine reflected, how often the memory of her first young husband and her first wedding day rose to her mind this morning. How very young she had been, and David too. She had felt shy and even panic-stricken. She felt neither of these things this morning. She was an experienced woman, well poised and sensible. The blind fervour of youth had given place to a far-seeing, more experienced love. How should it be otherwise when one was forty and had been married before?

David, the darling: he, too, had been young and a little shy. She could remember that after their wedding they had taken quite a time to get to know and understand one another. With Robert it would be different—they were both so much older, and already understood each other well. Undoubtedly a second marriage was easier and stood a better chance of succeeding. Not that the first hadn't been a great success, she went on thinking. But she could see now that wisdom . . . age . . . a deeper comprehension of life, were fine ingredients to bring to the construction of a perfect partnership.

Yesterday, down at the cottage, she and Mrs. Askell had moved the little walnut bureau and found behind it an old faded photograph of David in the uniform which he had worn in the R.A.M.C. in 1937. He had looked old-fashioned and sweet and rather pathetic.

She had put the photograph away in the box which already contained many souvenirs of her late husband, ready to be handed over to Pat and Judy. She had had a little conversation in her mind with David. She had said:

"You don't mind my doing this, do you?"

His answer had been:

"No, I'm glad. You've carried the burden of life alone far too long. I approve of what you are doing."

"You don't think I am wronging the children?"

"Certainly not. They are adults now and they have their own lives to lead. You owe something to yourself."

"And you approve of Robert, David?"

"One hundred per cent. I wouldn't wish to hand you over to a nicer chap."

"Then wish me luck, David."

And he had wished her luck from that Other World, and she had felt strangely at peace and contented in her memories of the past.

Now those memories would slip back into their rightful

place in the shadows, and she was to emerge into the sunshine of a new marriage . . . of her second husband's love.

Katherine drew a deep breath. She walked to the windows and looked out. The village of Cooltye lay bathed in the soft amber mist which betokened a warm day. She could see, silhouetted against the blue sky, the spire of St. Giles's Church, to which she would soon go forth to her wedding. Joyce and the vicar's wife had spent hours in there last night, doing the flowers. Some of the most beautiful of the roses on the altar had come from Katherine's own little garden. She would be sorry to say good-bye to those roses which she had tended for so long, but Robert had said that later she could take cuttings, and that he would buy her some more. But, in fact, she had felt quite a pang when she shut the gate of the Thatched Cottage behind her for the last time, knowing that it would now go up for sale along with any of its contents that Pat and Judy did not want.

The pang was not for herself. She could visualize a fuller and more attractive existence at Cooltye Farm. It was for Pat and Judy, who had not wished their home to be broken up nor to see it pass into strangers' hands.

Why, Katherine asked herself with a frown, must there always be *something* to spoil one's happiness? She wondered whether Judy realized how responsible she was, the hard little thing, for spoiling this great day for *her*.

They had had one conversation on the telephone during which Judy, in a bright, unrelenting voice, had said how well she was getting on in the shop, and how she loved working for her living and being independent. And the mother had been glad for her and yet longed for the one soft, affectionate word that did not come from Judy's lips. But at least she could be thankful Judy was all right, and Mrs. Chapman had very kindly written and confirmed the fact that the girl was "doing splendidly." Judy did not seem to worry about this impasse. It was Katherine who must needs fret.

Katherine sent a voiceless prayer across the sunlit fields in the direction of London.

"Judy, Judy, come down for my wedding. Please, please come down and make my day!"

Somebody knocked on her door.

"Come in," said Katherine, trying to banish the thought of her daughter.

In came Joyce with a tea-tray.

"Good morning, darling Katherine. And let me say all the formal things: *'Happy the bride the sun shines on'* and all that. Here are your letters."

Katherine seized them, putting on her horn-rimmed glasses (an ever constant reminder that a loss of accommodative power is one of the first signs of age). Hungrily she looked for a note from Judy and her heart leaped with gladness to find one written in the familiar big loopy writing. She tore it open, and Joyce, who also knew the handwriting, grimaced to herself. She still refused to be as tolerant about Judy's outlook as Bill was, and she couldn't *bear* the way Judy was punishing her mother because she wanted some happiness, apart from Miss Judy Green.

She saw Katherine's face fall. Quietly Katherine folded up the note.

"How typical of the young!" she said, with a light laugh which was obviously forced. "Now that everything's been packed up, Judy wants to know if I could find a couple of cushions to send her for her bed-sitting-room. Oh, well, I'll get Mrs. Askell to fish them out and post them off for me."

And nothing would induce her to let Joyce see how bitterly disappointed she was . . . because she had hoped that this letter was to say that Judy would be here this morning.

Joyce began to chatter merrily over their tea. Cooltye was seething with excitement, she said. Everybody was turning up at the church—even that sour old spinster, Miss Tomlinson, from the Dower House, Sir James and Lady Mallison from the Manor House—the biggest estate in the district—had sent their gardener down to the church early this morning with the most magnificent plants from their hothouse. Joyce had been up very early and received them.

"Oh, how kind!" exclaimed Katherine.

They were a nice couple, the Mallisons, and rather a sad pair, whose two sons had both been killed in the war, and who were condemned to spend the twilight of their lives without grandchildren, knowing that their possessions would pass into the hands of a nephew. How lucky *she* had been, thought Katherine, that Pat had been too young for that senseless, destructive war, and God grant there would never be another like it!

The Mallisons got all their farm produce from Robert, and Rob quite often went shooting with old Sir James. Rob and Katherine both had many such friends in the district, and received a surprising number of wedding presents, which one didn't really expect with a second marriage like hers.

Kindness from everybody, except Judy. . . .

"Oh, my darling," thought the mother, *"have I hurt you so much by this remarriage that you must retaliate remorselessly and be unkind to me? Oh, Judy, Judy, come down to my wedding, please."*

The next excitement was the arrival of Pat, who had had such a rush to get here that he was still in uniform. It always filled Katherine with tender humour and concern to see him in that badly fitting battledress. He was flushed and dusty, with grimy nails, but she hugged him with fierce mother-love, and whispered:

"Thank you for coming, Pat, you angel!"

"I hitch-hiked most of the way," he grinned. "Missed my train, and was afraid I'd miss the wedding."

"Oh, it's not for another couple of hours!" Katherine laughed. "I've got your clothes all ready, darling, in Bill's dressing-room. I'm sure Joyce won't mind if you pop into a bath."

She had just put on her blue silk dress. Her young son gazed at her admiringly.

"I say, Mum, you look a bit of all right!"

"Doesn't she!" seconded Joyce.

"Is Ju coming?"

The radiance left Katherine's eyes. She lowered her lashes. "I don't know."

"I don't expect she will," said Pat, with a slight cough of embarrassment. "She's still so bleak about you and Robert. She's a silly ass, and I told her so, but you know old Snub Nose when she gets a bee in her bonnet. Stubborn as a mule. Don't let it worry you, Mum."

"Oh, I don't . . . I don't!" cried Katherine in an unconvincing voice.

"She'll come round," added Pat.

"She'll come round." Everybody said that, but Katherine wondered how long it would be before Judy chose to surrender.

Pat said:

"Last time I spoke to her on the 'phone she was pretty busy in the shop and spending most of her spare time with Tony."

Katherine looked at him anxiously.

"She isn't going to be silly about Tony, is she?"

"Silly in what way, Mum?"

Katherine bit her lip.

"I mean . . . the boy is only a medical student and not even started on his career. I hope just because I'm getting married again that Judy won't rush into anything desperate."

"Oh, I shouldn't think so," said Pat, who was always vague about these matters and not vastly interested in his sister's little affair. He liked Tony Chapman. Thought him a good chap and all that.

He steered the conversation away from his sister.

"Can I get into the cottage . . . I mean after the wedding's over?"

Katherine looked anxious again.

"Oh, darling, it's all shut up. Was there something you wanted?"

He scratched his curly mop of hair.

"Oh, it doesn't matter. It was just, I thought I left a sports sweater . . . my Shrewsbury one . . . in my chest-of-drawers. I've got a chap who going to get some tennis going with me this summer in camp, and I wanted the sweater."

Katherine racked her memory. She and Mrs. Askell had found so many things belonging to the two children. Such a lot of rubbish which she had wanted to throw away, and yet not a single thing that belonged to them would she destroy without their permission. But Pat's sweater . . . *Had* she packed it?

"Oh, I believe it's in the case of your things which I

sent over with mine to the Farm, darling!" at length she said.

Pat remained silent. He was thinking that "it was a bind" not being able to go home as usual and find his own room full of his things. It would really want getting used to, this switch-over to Cooltye Farm.

Fearfully, Katherine looked at her son's face. She knew his every expression so well. She could see that he was troubled.

"Pat, darling, you didn't mind my packing up for you and sending your things to the Farm? You see, the cottage is up for sale, and when you come home for your next leave it will be to Robert's place. You don't *mind*, do you?"

The boy was too sensitive and soft-hearted to damp her spirits by answering truthfully in that moment. He did mind, almost as much as Judy, but he wanted his adored mother of his to be happy. The change would just want a bit of getting used to, he told himself. But he was sure it would work out all right. One of his Army pals had a stepfather and they got on like a house on fire. No reason why *he* shouldn't get on with Robert once they were accustomed to the new relationship.

So he said:

"I don't mind a bit, Mum. You can get hold of the old sweater some time and post it to camp for me."

He was rewarded by seeing her brow grow clear again. Then he went off for his bath and Katherine to finish her *toilette*, while Joyce rushed round the house. Bill had finished his morning round and was "togging up," as he called it. The friend who was minding the children was getting little Katherine washed and dressed; she could hear her screams of laughter. Nicholas was to be allowed to walk beside baby's pram, stand outside the church and watch the bride and bridegroom come out. He had his little bag of confetti all ready to throw at Godmother, which was a huge excitement.

Katherine at her dressing-table put on the big white hat, which made a perfect frame for the sun-tanned, lovely face. Her fingers trembled a little. She laughed at herself. Was the woman of forty going to get "nerves" after all . . . like the girl of twenty years ago? She reddened her lips—put a pin in a truant wave of shining hair.

Still not a sign of Judy . . . not even a telephone call or a telegram (and there had been lots of telegrams already from friends who couldn't come today). She had had a personal letter of good wishes from her publisher, too (he had actually sent her a lovely little bedside radio for a wedding present). But *nothing* from Judy.

Katherine glanced at the clock. A little more than an hour to the wedding. It would all have been so heavenly if she could have had Judy in the car with her as well as Pat and Joyce.

"Perhaps I'm asking too much," she told herself humbly, and the tears suddenly stung her eyes. She could not *bear* this estrangement from her young daughter.

But she tried to tell herself that there was still time. *She might come . . . she might.*

But one hour later, when she was in the car with Bill (resplendent in a morning suit which he openly declared had belonged to an uncle, and fitted him ill), Judy had not turned up. So it was with an ache in her heart that Katherine Green set out for her wedding to Robert Tracy and the sting of unshed tears behind her eyes.

Bill Haddon, full of good cheer, stole a look at the face of the woman he had loved long ago, and who still commanded his deepest respect and admiration. To him she looked like the Katherine of his youth—so youthful and exquisite was that fine, intelligent face under the big white hat. She carried a posy of beautiful white roses which Robert had sent her. Bill said:

"This is a great day for you, Kate."

He hadn't called her that for years. The old nickname brought a smile to her lips, and she held out her hand to him.

"I'm very happy, Bill. But I wish Judy had come."

Secretly, Dr. Haddon felt he could have spanked young Judy, and yet the psychologist in him had to find some excuse for her. The poor kid . . . on this day when Robert Tracy was getting his heart's desire, Judy was losing her mother, *"say what you like"*, Bill soliloquized. *"Katherine can never*

*again give undivided love and attention to Judy. She'll belong
three-quarters, anyhow, to her husband . . . and rightly. But
one can see the thing from the kid's angle."*

He wanted to spank her, however, because she might have
made an effort for Katherine on this day of days.

The sun was shining and the sky a clear blue, and a little
crowd of villagers had gathered outside St. Giles's to watch
the bride arrive. She could see them lining the path that led
from the lych gate past the old tombstones, right up to the
church door. Bill gave her a hand, and as she stepped out
the little crowd raised a murmur:

"There she is, bless her heart . . ."

"Don't she look grand . . ."

"My, she looks young, does Mrs. Green today!"

And Katherine, heart beating fast and her whole soul
thrilling to the occasion, smiled and greeted her friends of
Cooltye and murmured:

"Thank you."

She mustn't think about Judy, now. She was going to meet
Robert, her bridegroom. Today was *his* and hers—theirs
alone.

The organ swelled gently. The little church was packed.
Sunshine slanted through the stained-glass windows. The
altar roses filled the air with rich fragrance. The first person
whom Katherine saw was her son, spruce and with a white
buttonhole, doing his job as usher. She smiled at him. And
then, suddenly, her heart gave a lurch, and the whole world
became perfect for her. *For Judy was there!* Judy, in a pew
right at the back of the church, but she was there, wearing
a familiar grey flannel suit (and an unfamiliar white hat
which she must have bought for the occasion!). As her mother
passed Judy gave her a nervous smile, her hands gripping
her prayer book. Katherine smiled back with deepest gratitude, and her lips formed the words:

"Judy, my darling . . ."

She saw none of the other faces turned so admiringly
towards her. Everything now seemed a little hazy until she
reached Robert's side. How tall he was! And he did not look
at all embarrassed, but quite self-possessed (he, too, in bor-
rowed finery . . . the black coat and striped trousers suited

him, even though it made him look a little older than the Robert in his corduroys and shirt). His dark hair was stiffly brushed, and a shaft of sunlight fell upon him, showing up the silver wings over each ear. His deep-set eyes smiled down at her and he took her hand, which was shaking slightly, and held it in a strong, protective clasp. It seemed to Katherine symbolic of the strength, the protection that he was going to afford her for the rest of his life.

Michael Cairn stood beside him, resplendent in Naval uniform, which added a decided touch of glamour. He looked more nervous than the bridegroom, Pat afterwards told his mother.

Now Mr. Jenners approached them, benignly smiling, fingering his stole. The organ trembled into silence. Not a sound could be heard in the church. Mr. Jenners, in his nice, modulated voice, began:

"Dearly beloved, we are gathered here together . . ."

In the back pew Katherine's children watched. Pat felt a little emotional. His long-lashed blue eyes gravely regarded the slim, beautiful back of the bride, who was now making her responses:

"I, Katherine Judith Green, take thee, Robert Bingham Tracy . . ."

Pat thought:

"I hope it's a success for Mum's sake. I wonder what Dad would have said. . . ."

But Judy, staring at that familiar back with brilliant eyes which held a trace of bitterness, was thinking in a much more complicated manner. And the first irrelevant reflection was:

"I didn't even know Uncle Robert's name was Bingham . . ."

And then:

"I wish I hadn't come. I wish I hadn't been so soft. Oh, I can't bear it! To listen to her promising to share everything with him, become his goods and chattels until she dies . . . I just loathe it!"

Her insensate, irrational dislike of Robert Tracy increased as she listened to him quietly promising to love and cherish her mother.

"He can become her lord and master if he likes, but he's not going to boss me. . . ."

Now Judy was thankful that she could kneel down with the rest of the congregation and hide her face in her hands, because she was crying. She snuffled into her handkerchief. The thought of Tony alone supported her. She would always have *him* even though she had lost Mummy. Later on (so they had decided when they talked things over) they would announce the fact that they wanted to get married and ask Mummy's consent. And Judy meant to see that Robert Tracy didn't have a say in it. . . .

Pat heard the snuffles and whispered:

"Shut up, Snub Nose. Don't be an ass. It isn't as bad as all that."

She did not answer him. She felt that she had even lost some of her brother's affection through Robert Tracy. She had only come down because at the very last moment she had relented and darling Tony had suggested that she might regret it all her life because of the public snub to Mummy. So here she was. But not for long. The moment the ceremony was over she was off back to town. She couldn't even face the reception. She *couldn't.* Having to play a part as happy little Judy, welcoming nice kind stepfather and listening to all the congratulations, then seeing Mummy go off on her honeymoon with *him.*

Then the wedding was over. Judy watched her mother walking down the aisle on Robert's arm to the triumphant strains of the "Wedding March." The church bells were pealing. Mummy's face looked rather wonderful, Judy grudgingly admitted, with that light in her eyes; and certainly in that big white hat and the new blue get-up she might have been Judy's sister. Judy threw a slanting glance at the bridegroom. He was smiling. To Judy he looked smug and self-satisfied. She grew taut again.

"He's got her," she said to herself with furious resentment. *"He's taken her from Pat and me. Oh, I hate him!"*

Now the bridal group had to be marshalled for the local photographers. One or two cameramen had come in from Brighton because these two were "news"—Robert being a well-known and prosperous gentleman farmer, and Katherine Green an authoress.

Judy avoided the camera. Just before the bride and bridegroom stepped into their waiting car Katherine anxiously searched for her daughter, saw her and beckoned.

"See you and Pat at Mulberry House, darling."

Quickly Judy said:

"So sorry, Mummy. I can't. Please forgive me. I've got to go straight to the station and back to my job."

Robert looked at the pretty, flushed face of his newly acquired stepdaughter. Gently he said:

"Your mother and I will be very disappointed if you are not at the reception, Judy."

She gave him a hard, glittering smile.

"Most kind of you, but, as it is—I had some difficulty in getting away from my job for the wedding, and I must get back."

The newly made Mrs. Robert Tracy flung her daughter a pleading look.

"Judy darling. Can't you even spare half an hour?"

"Out of the question, Mummy. But it was lovely being at the wedding, and all my best wishes and all that," said Judy with unnatural formality. Then bent, touched her mother's cheek, turned and was gone, lost in the crowd.

Once again the radiance for Katherine was dimmed. But Robert put an arm round her and led her to the car, with its white bridal ribbons.

"Come along, darling. We must get on. . . ."

She pulled herself together and smiled at him. She was his wife. Once again she reminded herself that this was *his* day, and she was so very very lucky and happy, too. At least Judy had come to the wedding. She must not ask too much of life—or Judy!

She sat down in the car, smiling, shaking a little with emotion, her hand tight-clasped in her husband's.

Little Nicholas Haddon skipped up to the car and flung his precious confetti over Katherine, screaming:

"Aunty Katrine, Aunty Katrine!"

Katherine brushed away the confetti and waved at the

child. The car moved on. Once out of sight of the crowd, Robert took his beautiful bride in his arms. Now there was no room in her heart or mind for anything but him, as she surrendered to his kiss.

8

It is a sad fact that the English climate cannot be relied upon to give a sunny welcome even to the most patriotic of English people who return from a trip to the Continent.

Mr. and Mrs. Robert Tracy flew back from Paris, *en route* from their Austrian honeymoon—both deeply tanned by the sunshine—and drove home in Robert's car, which his head man, Armstrong, had brought to Hassock's Station to meet them, in the pouring rain.

It was such a bad day that Katherine had to laugh. The sweet Sussex countryside was hidden in a dark grey mist, with storm clouds racing across a frowning sky. The Downs looked sombre and even menacing. It was also very cold, and Katherine was glad of her traveling coat.

"It's been like this for the last ten days," Armstrong informed them gloomily. "The lanes are so rutted up with mud the cart-wheels are sticking in them, and it's a poor prospect for haymaking."

Robert laughed.

"Oh, you ought to know our climate better than to talk like that, Joe. There'll be a sudden change and brilliant sunshine, perhaps, tomorrow."

As they drove along the familiar road towards Cooltye, Katherine slipped a hand round her husband's arm and sat back with a contented sigh. The dismal weather made no impression upon her. It was good to see the old country and Sussex again, even on this cold, stormy day. She felt as she looked—superlatively well. She had had two such glorious weeks as Robert's bride, nothing could depress her. She looked up at him with a glance which was still as shy as a girl's and yet held all the tenderness of maturity.

"It's been wonderful, Rob, hasn't it?" she murmured.

His fingers pressed hers.

"Quite unforgettable, darling. And quite apart from us —it's made me wonder why I've been so conservative in the past about my holidays. All very well, bathing in Cornwall or golfing at Broadstairs, but my word . . . those mountains . . . that lake . . ."

"And that sun!" she finished with a laugh.

Then they were silent, absorbed in their reflections.

For Katherine, the soft blurred line of the Downs was replaced suddenly by the majesty of the mighty Austrian mountains, and that superb emerald-green lake in Rosenhauer. The almost unearthly brilliance of it—not only in the sunlight, but in the white radiance of the moon. The fairy-tale silhouette of the Schloss. Their bedroom with the balcony on which they used to sit and eat their breakfast with the sun already warm upon their faces.

Every day they had walked miles and miles . . . taking their lunch in their rucksacks. She had picked armfuls of wild flowers, intoxicated by their beauty. They had both been charmed by the simplicity of the peasants . . . their kindliness . . . their eagerness to please. They had eaten good food and drunk good wine. They had grown young and, with the return to youth, experienced all its vital happiness and tireless energy. Yet, as Robert had told her, all the fresh air, which was like champagne—and the strenuous exercise —had not prevented her from putting on weight. Her cheeks had filled out a little and she looked even younger today, he declared, than when she had left Cooltye, two weeks ago. Nobody in the hotel would believe that she had a grown-up son in the Army. They had thought her a girl, whose fair hair was growing prematurely grey.

As for Robert, he, too, had "filled out a little, and his finely cut, bony face wore a new look of boyish good humour and contentment which Katherine had never really seen upon it before.

In other words, Katherine reflected as they drove through the gates of Cooltye Farm, their honeymoon had been a complete success. Perhaps a bigger success than even she had dared hope, because it had been a great adventure (were not all marriages a leap into the dark?) . . . Robert might have disappointed her. After all, she had the most tender memories of David, her first husband—Robert had had a lot to live up to. But he had come out of it triumphant. She had found him a charming lover as well as the most considerate of husbands. As for their companionship . . . she had always known that would be all right.

She had felt proud of him and almost smugly self-satisfied out there in that lakeside hotel, where there were younger couples who seemed to Katherine far less content with each other. One young English pair appeared frankly bored. The girl, half Katherine's age and reminding her a little poignantly of Judy, was also there on her honeymoon, but seemed to spend most of the time fighting with her young husband. He was an aggressive, selfish youngster—no doubt in love with his youthful bride—but he had a poor way of showing it. He had a mania for cars and had a racing Bugatti in which he took himself off, roaring daily down the *autobahn*. But she stayed behind because she loved to walk, or to bathe, quietly. They fought openly during meals and once Katherine had found the girl in the garden, crying her eyes out.

"Rupert's a selfish pig!" she had stormed, opening her heart to Katherine.

How sorry Katherine had felt for her, and how pleased with her husband; dear Rob, who not only liked to do the things that she did, but would not have dreamed of doing anything else without asking her first. On all occasions he put himself second. She had even remonstrated with him one evening.

Robert was a fine bridge-player. He had been asked by three other men in the hotel to make up a fourth. He had absolutely refused because he would not leave Katherine alone.

"Darling, you mustn't spoil me!" she protested. "I'm quite used to sitting back while Pat and Judy do what they want, and I can always read a book—or write one!"

He had said:

"Nothing doing. This is where you get priority, my Kath.

And I haven't the slightest wish to play bridge with these chaps."

She was quite certain that he would have enjoyed the game, and loved him for his consideration.

"But you do spoil me," she had protested on another occasion.

And his reply had been:

"Surely it's a man's privilege to be able to spoil the woman he loves!"

Lying in his arms that night, listening to music coming across the lake in the warm beauty of the Austrian night, she had felt humbly grateful to Providence for giving her this second chance in life—for giving her a man like Robert Tracy.

But even at that earthly paradise at Rosenhauer, the small serpent of unhappiness had managed to wriggle its way in once or twice, and destroy the utter perfection. For Judy did not write to her mother. Pat sent two long letters, one from camp, where he was under canvas and enjoying manœuvres. He hoped she was having a good time and looked forward to seeing her when she got back. He even remembered to put a P.S. *"Regards to Robert"*.

But from Judy not a line.

Katherine had written to them both; two letters and many postcards. Those colourful ones with lots of exotic stamps which they had always liked to receive from their friends abroad. She had bought them many presents. A heavenly Austrian embroidered blouse for Judy. A beer-mug that played a tune for Pat.

Wherever she went with Robert . . . strolling through the little shops in the mountain villages or in the towns . . . she had felt the mother-love in her rushing to the fore . . . she kept seeing things which she thought would please them.

"Just what Judy adores . . ." or *"How Pat would like that!"*

Robert had smiled at her on several occasions and said:

"How you do love those two, bless you, Kath!"

Yes, she loved them. With the greatest and most passionate of all loves . . . a mother's absorbing devotion. But there was bitterness in the thought that Judy could go on hurting her like this. And because Katherine could not help seeing the other side . . . always there was that lingering doubt in her heart as to whether she had taken this great happiness with Robert at Judy's expense.

Seeing some of those young girls growing brown and strong in the mountain sunlight, or diving into the crystal lake, she had secretly hungered for Judy—wished she could be there to enjoy it, too, like those others of her age. It wasn't a very pleasant thing to remember that Judy was slaving away for her living in a London shop—with nowhere to go, even for weekends. Judy, who so loved country life. Yet when she had voiced these thoughts to Robert he had reminded her gently that it was Judy's own fault.

"She knows she's only got to turn up at the Farm and she'll be more than welcome."

Of course he was right, so Katherine had no more to say. But silently grieved and wondered how she could make Judy forgive her this "crime."

But the home-coming to Cooltye Farm was not to be allowed by the Fates to be by any means perfect. Scarcely had they covered a mile or two from the station before Armstrong broke the news that Mrs. Bunting would not be there to welcome them. Robert had sent instructions that she was to cook the evening meal, but she had visited Armstrong in person this morning and told him that she would not be going to the Farm any more, and would he tell Mr. Robert so.

Robert gave a wry smile and turned an apologetic gaze upon his wife.

"Sorry, darling! The old So-and-So! But I really thought she'd hang on until we got home. We'll have to find a couple at once."

Armstrong, who was a hard-working, honest chap without much humour, was bent on being gloomy today—in keeping with the weather.

Armstrong interrupted:

"She never meant to turn up, did that woman. Jealous of Mr. Robert's marriage—that is it."

Robert laughed and gently fingered one of Katherine's hands.

"Never mind, we'll manage."

"There's always my faithful Mrs. Askell——" began Katherine.

"Pardon me, ma'am, but when I got Mr. Robert's telegram I went straight to her, but even *she* can't come. Not because she doesn't want to, but she's laid up with the lumbago and can't move, poor creature."

Katherine was all concern for her old "daily." She then made light of the fact that she was returning to a house in which there were no servants.

"You ought to know what a good cook I am, Rob. I can manage," she said gaily.

It was Robert's turn to look with gloom upon the stormy landscape.

They were just rounding a bend in the road and could now see the beautiful, lichen-covered rooftops of the Farm. Despite the beauty of the Austrian scenery, and quite apart from his great happiness with Katherine, Robert had found it a little too exotic for his taste. He had looked forward to seeing Cooltye again. He was proud of his farm; the lovely old house . . . the green pastures . . . the grazing cattle and those fine new modern cowsheds with all their electrical equipment; the big dairy which could not have been bettered anywhere. He even liked the rain—the soft blurred landscape of his beloved Sussex. But he had meant to have a celebration dinner on this first night home with his wife. He did not wish her to be in the kitchen, cooking, and doing the washing-up.

But Katherine insisted that she did not mind and that they would soon find somebody. She would put an advertisement in the local paper tomorrow and write to an agency she knew in Horsham.

Armstrong, who was a goodly man (himself unmarried and with little interest in the weaker sex), looked with respectful if reluctant admiration at the new Mrs. Robert Tracy, when he opened the door for her to get out of the car. He had always heard her spoken well of in Cooltye, and he thought her a fine-looking woman, but he himself was a bit put out by this marriage. Mr. Robert was a wonderful employer—a gentleman with no class prejudice. Many a night they used to have a beer and a game of darts together in the "local." All that would stop now, with Mrs. Robert to keep him at home.

Katherine walked into the house, which struck very cold despite the fact that Armstrong himself had lit a fire in the kitchen and in the living-room. The central heating had still to be installed. There had been no time before the wedding. But the decorations had been completed and it all looked really most exciting, Katherine thought as, with hands in her coat pocket and fair hair uncovered, she walked round examining everything. She was pleased to see some of her own things—dear, familiar objects from the little Thatched Cottage. And it would all look still better when she had the new curtains and covers made up, she reflected.

There were roses—a magnificent bunch of them—in a bowl on the high, carved-wood mantelpiece, and they found more flowers in their bedroom. These, Armstrong said, had been brought down and arranged by "the doctor's wife." Dear Joyce's work. And a card which said:

"Welcome home to the bride and bridegroom"

and a little note to the effect that she was keeping the two Corgis, Pip and Squeak, which she had been looking after while their mistress was on her honeymoon, until the morrow, and that if Katherine liked to ring her up she would explain why, as she had meant to have them here all ready to leap into Katherine's arms.

When Katherine 'phoned, Joyce told her that when she had come round early in the day, bringing the dogs with her, Sally, Robert's collie, had been very unpleasant and had even started a fight with Pip, so she had decided that it would not be a good thing to keep the dogs shut up together alone —before anybody was in the house.

Katherine put down the receiver and wrinkled her nose. She had feared that Sally might resent the intruders. The Collie had just rushed to the gates, barking madly with delight when Robert had appeared, and she was now at his heels. Well, Katherine reflected, she must be patient and trust that Sally would in time learn to accept the Corgis. She would go over to Mulberry House and fetch Pip and Squeak tomorrow. But she was a little disappointed not to see her own pets here tonight.

However, that was a small "fly in the ointment" and she wasn't going to let it worry her unduly.

There were a pile of letters waiting on the hall table. Eagerly Katherine went through them, sitting by the fire while Robert brought her a glass of sherry to bring some warmth back into her cold body. A postcard from Pat, the darling. Nothing sentimental, but all that she wanted . . . a reminder of his affection, and say: *"Hope to get leave in about ten days' time and will come down if Robert says it's O.K."*

That gave her a little pang. *"If Robert say it's O.K."* She didn't want Pat ever to doubt that he would be welcome here. She did so hope that he would be accustomed to spending his leaves at the Farm just as naturally as he used to do at the Thatched Cottage. She would hate him to hesitate for a moment on that score.

Ah! Judy *had* written! Sipping her sherry, and with the firelight bringing a glow to her bronzed face, Katherine scanned Judy's note. But it was stilted, and written as though under compulsion . . . as though the girl's better self had dictated it, but that other unforgiving side forbade that it should show a hint of surrender.

"Dearest Mummy,

Just to say I hope you had a good holiday and have come back very fit. When do you begin a new book? I saw an advert of that last one of yours, and hope it sells well.

I'm O.K. and working very hard. We did a wedding last week . . . lots of fun. I made the bridesmaids' posies, and Liza did the bride's bouquet. Everyone seemed very pleased, and I think there's another wedding in the offing. Tony and I queued for the pit for the new Christopher Fry, which we both thought jolly good.

Must fly.

Much love,

Judy."

Katherine let the letter fall on to her lap and lit a cigarette. Her eyelids narrowed as she smoked and reflected. She could hear Robert's footsteps in the room above. He was changing. Armstrong particularly wanted him to go down to the Farm for half an hour. He hadn't wanted to leave her, but of course she had told him he must go.

"I'm going to be a good farmer's wife, darling," she had laughed, "and learn to take second place to your job."

He had kissed her with that warm passion which was now so necessary and deeply fulfilling, and said:

"You will never take second place to anything, Kath. You will be first with me in everything from now onward."

She believed him. But she was thinking about her young daughter now. She glanced through the letter again. A pleasant little note on the surface. But Katherine knew her Judy . . . she was not the literary type . . . not at all like her mother, who wrote very long, expansive letters to the children. But there could have been so much *more* in that "welcome home" note. It showed so conclusively that Judy was pleased to be dutiful, but determined on no further capitulation. She would wish her mother well, and let her know that *she* was well, but that note lacked all the old spontaneous affection which Katherine had prized. Once she would have said *"I've missed you dreadfully, Mum"* or, *"Simply can't wait to see you again."* But there was nothing like that.

Katherine suddenly decided that she would take her cue from Judy. She had never, she told herself wryly, learned not to be too "soft." So, with her coat still on, she went into the dining-room and through to the small room which Robert used to use as a kind of "den." He rarely sat in it, so he had insisted upon giving it to her and calling it by the grander name of "study." Here were her own desk and her typewriter, her manuscripts and books, ready waiting to be sorted.

Once again Katherine felt pleased by these familiar objects, and pleased with her Robert, who so understood her needs. She sat down at the typewriter and typed a little note to Judy.

"Thanks, darling, for yours, and so glad all's well with you. I've got you an embroidered peasant's blouse and will

*post it to you tomorrow, and only hope we shall get some
summer so that you can wear it."*

She paused a moment. With all the love and longing in
her heart she wanted to beg and implore Judy to come down
and "make it up" with Robert and put things right for *her*.
But she tilted her head and added the words:

*"Pat hopes to get leave in ten days' time, and come down
to the Farm. It would be rather jolly if you could snatch a
holiday from your flower shop and join us."*

"It would be rather jolly!"

What a masterly understatement! It would be wonderful
. . . all that Katherine needed to make life perfect. But she
would not say so, would not do any more about Judy than
this. The girl must make the first move.

An hour later Katherine was washed and had changed
into well-cut, plum-coloured slacks and a pale blue jersey
which, moulded to her slim figure, made her look like a girl.
Robert was enchanted when he saw her thus attired, wander-
ing round his big, freshly painted kitchen, examining pots
and pans.

It was raining again. He was soaked, and had come in
wiping the drops from his face. Appreciatively he regarded
Katherine and spread his hands to the kitchen stove.

"It's mighty nice in here," he said. "And I've got a
mighty nice-looking cook-housekeeper, I *must* say."

Katherine laughed, and peered into the larder.

"Joyce did the shopping. I've just been on the 'phone to
her. I see there are some chops and there's plenty of cheese.
I make rather a good cheese savoury. How about it?"

"Just bread and cheese will do for me," said Robert.
"Don't tire yourself cooking tonight."

"But I *want* to. And I'm not going to let you eat bread
and cheese. You're too used to fine living in Austria, my
sweet!"

He walked up to her, took her in his arms and buried his
face against her golden tanned throat.

"You're a lovely thing, Kath," he whispered. "And what

100

is more you're efficient and practical. What else can any man ask in his wife? I'm rather glad Mrs. Bunting didn't turn up. It's rather fun having you all alone tonight."

"I was thinking the same," she said almost shyly. "Don't let's go into the dining-room. This is such a lovely kitchen. I always have adored the beams and all your copper pots and pans and your blue-willow china. We might still be in our Austrian paradise. I'll put a cloth on this table and we'll be the real farmer and his wife and have our food in here."

"I can think of nothing I'd like better," said Robert, and hugged her.

While he took off his wet boots, pipe in his mouth, he watched the slim figure in the slacks and jersey moving round, busy preparing the evening meal. She looked happy doing it and that was all that mattered. Glamorous though she was, his Katherine did not demand luxury, or find servants essential to her happiness. She was a woman who obviously extracted a great deal of pleasure out of doing things for other people. He admired her as profoundly as he loved her. He said:

"Any letters worth reading?"

"Pat may be coming down at the end of next week."

"Good," he said with a pleasure he felt.

The name "Judy" hovered in the air between them a little dangerously, but was left unspoken. Robert presumed that there could be no news from *her*—because Katherine did not mention her. However, she seemed in radiant good spirits during the meal, which they ate in their warm kitchen, listening to the rain lashing against the casements, as though it were a winter night. Dear Katherine! Robert thought, she might grieve for Judy, but she was not going to show it to him. But he did not want her to be repressed or to fear that he would find any mention of her children aggravating.

Much later, when they were upstairs and Katherine was brushing her ash-blonde hair, he put his hands on her shoulders and looked at her reflection in the mirror. Seeing her there, in one of her filmy nightgowns and the pale blue satin dressing-gown which were part of her hurriedly bought trousseau, was an immense thrill for him. He could still hardly believe that this lovely woman was his wife, and that after so many long, lonely years in this house he would have her always here—they would spend many such an evening as they had just spent . . . together . . . homely and content . . . they would always share this room, which was full of Katherine's pretty, feminine things; and he would enjoy all the rapture of loving and being loved which he had never known before. It was not perhaps such a novelty for her, she had already been a wife. Yet he knew, because she had told him so out in Austria, that she was utterly *his*, and that he had no cause to be jealous even of memories connected with the husband she had loved and lost. At the same time, he did not wish to be jealous, either, of the love she bore the children.

"Kath, darling," he said gently, "wasn't there a letter from Judy?"

He saw her flush and that sweet mouth harden a little.

"Yes. But no news, except that she seems to be getting on quite well with her job."

He kissed the top of her head.

"I'll drop the child a line myself when I get a second and tell her I'd like her to come down," he said quietly.

Katherine turned to him, and for a moment, with her arms round his waist, leaned her head against his breast and hugged him to her.

"You're a *darling*, Robert. A darling, understanding person. . . . I just adore you!"

Later on—lying in his arms in the great four-poster bed, listening to the creaking of the boughs, tossed by the gale, outside in the garden, and to the continued lash of rain—she felt humbly grateful for her happiness and for such a man as this one.

But when she fell asleep it was with the provocative thought of her young daughter in her mind's eye . . . hurtful . . . embittering a little the sweets of this second marriage. And she knew that she must resign herself to the inevitable and positive fact that she was still very much Judy's mother, as well as Robert's wife.

9

ABOUT three weeks later, on one of those hot, airless August evenings in London when the rooftops seemed to merge into a grey haze of heat, somebody tapped on Judy Green's bed-sitting-room door. A voice said:

"Can I come in a moment?"

Judy had been sitting on the edge of her bed with a pad on her knee, writing to her brother. He had just sent her one of his rare notes to say that he was off any moment to Languard Fort, near Felixstowe, for rifle practice. He was snatching a "48," down at Cooltye, as from Friday, and wanted Judy to meet him for a snack in town.

She had just written to him:

"You may as well know before you come up, Pat darling, that Tony and I are engaged. Tony is telling his people. I haven't seen them yet, but hope it'll be all right. We want to get married straight away because Tony sees no object in my living alone any more. The difficulty is Mummy; she might object, as I'm sure she'll think I'm rushing into marriage because of what's happened at home, and it isn't true. I know Tony isn't very old yet, but he's approaching his Finals and they all say he's brilliant, and after all he'll get a Government grant of about £3 a week which will help. Thank goodness he's finished with his National Service, so we won't have a parting to fear. . . ."

That was as far as she had got. She had only been back from the shop an hour, but she had written to her mother. The bulky envelope was already addressed and stamped, waiting to be posted. She had told Mummy all about it, and sunk her pride sufficiently to *beg* for the "permit," as she called it. Assured her that she knew her own mind, and had always loved Tony, etc., etc.

She opened the door, cheeks flushed a trifle guiltily. She had recognized the voice of her friend Elizabeth. Now for the peroration! Liza would have been home and heard the news from *her* people.

One look at Elizabeth's face and Judy's heart sank. It was not a smiling one. Elizabeth looked anxious and upset. She was a tall girl, as fair as Tony was dark, although with the same almond-shaped eyes—blue in her case—and she wore her hair very short, cropped like a fair cap. She looked older than her brother, although she was actually his junior. She had many of his good qualities of industry, and devotion to any job which she was doing, but she was more easily harassed. What Tony himself called "temperamental."

Judy, who knew her well, thought that she was in one of her temperamental moods at this very moment. At such times she could be quite brusque—without any of her ordinary charm.

"I say, Judy, you are a so-and-so!" she began bluntly, and looked at the younger girl with angry blue eyes.

Immediately Judy knew that *she* knew.

Elizabeth added:

"There's been a scene at home. Tony has told Mamma and Pop that he wants to marry you at once—if your mother consents. There's been a family conference and the result is that Pop looks like a thunder cloud and Mummy's gone off to her bridge wailing that Tony's future will be ruined. And what *I* feel rather upset about is that you haven't said a *word* to me."

Judy was crimson now to the roots of her curly hair. She looked at her friend with genuine distress.

"Oh, Liza! I'm dreadfully sorry. Sit down . . . here . . ." gulping, she pulled a chair forward for her friend. Elizabeth flung herself into it; despite the fact that she was wearing a thin summer frock she looked and felt hot and cross. She said:

"So you ought to be."

Then Judy prepared for battle.

"I don't quite see why. I didn't tell you because Tony asked me not to until we had settled things in our own minds. I *wanted* to tell you."

Elizabeth pulled a packet of cigarettes from her pocket and lit one.

"Well, Tony's pretty mean not to have taken me into his confidence."

"We thought it better to say nothing until we had finally decided."

"How long has this been going on?" Elizabeth asked sulkily.

"About a month, I suppose."

"Well, I knew you both went out a lot and were having a sort of 'affair,' but I didn't imagine you meant anything like an immediate marriage."

Judy coloured again, her fingers nervously folding the half-finished letter to her brother.

"We're terribly in love, Liza. I do hope you'll forgive us. You've been such a brick to me. I'd die if I thought *you* thought me ungrateful going behind your back and so on."

Elizabeth looked at her friend's pretty, troubled face, and her lips softened. She had had a few arguments with Judy in the past. No two girls could work together all day and every day and see eye to eye all the time. Both of them had strong, rather self-assertive natures. At the same time, Elizabeth, being the older, had always felt somewhat responsible for Judy—more particularly so because she had persuaded her to leave home and come up here. But it had never entered her head that *this* would be the result.

Judy said:

"I thought you all rather . . . liked me, in the family." The words were stammered. . . . "I didn't know you would loathe the idea of my being Tony's wife."

Now Elizabeth's face relaxed still more. Judy was a darling, really. There was something awfully sweet and "honest-to-God" about her.

"Don't be silly . . . we don't loathe the idea . . . it isn't that at all. Personally, I'd like to have you for a sister-in-law. It's just that I felt hurt because you've been arranging it all behind my back."

"But I didn't mean that at all, Liza!" said Judy earnestly.

"It was just that we wanted to be *sure* before we came into the open. Now we are certain. That's all."

"Oh, well," said Elizabeth gloomily, and added, "I can't imagine Tony as a married man."

"But he's old for his age, really, Liza. He's terribly self-possessed and dependable. You'll agree with that!"

"Yes, but he hasn't even qualified yet. He's got another year...."

"But it doesn't have to interfere at all with his work . . . our getting married, I mean. He'll carry on at Bart's just as usual."

"Oh, I dare say it'll be all right," Elizabeth conceded, growing more accustomed to the idea and conscious that it would be really rather nice to have one of her best friends as a sister-in-law. She herself in fact, had argued on Judy's side when the family storm broke over Tony's head. Tony might have chosen somebody very much worse than Judy Green, who had a charming mother and had had a good education and who obviously adored Tony, she had declared.

Elizabeth told Judy now what had been said at home. And the main purport of it was, of course, that Judy was too young and that Tony ought to wait until he had qualified and was in a settled practice.

Judy, feeling exhausted and miserable after she had talked to Elizabeth a bit longer, raised a pair of rather tragic eyes to her friend.

"Am I going to be barred from your house in future? Won't your mother want to see me any more?"

"Don't be an idiot," said Elizabeth. "Of course she will. She's very fond of you, and so is Pop. They won't object to an engagement. I expect they'll just try and stop you marrying so soon, that's all."

"But they can't!" said Judy quickly.

"No, they can't, and Tony let them know pretty definitely that whatever they say, he's going through with it," admitted Elizabeth.

Judy's good spirits returned. She felt a thrill of pride. How passionately she loved Tony! How enormously she admired him! She said:

"Elizabeth, I assure you Tony and I have talked this thing

over *ad nauseam* and always reached the same conclusion . . . that as we love each other and feel so dead sure . . . we might just as well have a little home together while we go on with our jobs, even if it means cheap digs until Tony gets ahead a bit more."

"I think it's rather plucky of you," admitted Elizabeth. "I'm not sure I'm not rather jealous. You certainly must love Tony an awful lot. I wouldn't want to begin marriage without a bit of money and security . . ." she gave a short laugh . . . "perhaps I'm more mercenary than you are, although I never realized until now that *you* were so romantic."

"Well, I hope I'm not romantic to the point of being sick-making," said Judy hurriedly, with her usual wish to cover up her deepest emotions, "but I must say money doesn't count much with Tony and me. We've got just enough between us to live on—that is if you'll let me go on at *Fleurette*."

"Of course I will. Now I've had instructions from Tony to take you back to supper," said Elizabeth, getting up and looking out at the hot summer sky. "I left him in his bath. He said he needed cooling down after Mamma's tirade! This weather's atrocious; it's making us all irritable. I am sorry I started off by being so disagreeable, Judy darling. I'm *really* on your side."

Judy's eyes grew big and bright.

"Oh, Liza, I'm terribly glad to hear you say that. All the way along I've thought it would be so grand to have you for a sister-in-law. Oh, Liza, *dare* I face the family this evening?"

Elizabeth patted Judy's shoulder.

"Of course! I know the family. I think Pop has a very soft spot for you, and so has Mamma really. It'll all end in everyone kissing everyone else and Pop opening a bottle. It's just that we've got to persuade them to believe that Tony's career isn't going to be ruined by marriage."

"It *can't* be if we both stick to our jobs and don't have children too soon," said Judy, with the optimism of her years.

Elizabeth suddenly threw her friend a penetrating look.

"All this business of *our* side is all very well. What about *your* mother! It's you who are under age. Will Mrs. Green . . . I mean Mrs. Tracy . . . give her consent?"

Now Judy felt her whole body stiffen. The light left her eyes. It was as though that switch-over from the name of Green to Tracy was a sharp jab, reminding her of her mother's new status. It fell like a stone wall between her and her happiness.

She picked up the long letter she had written her mother. "I've just written for the consent. Here it is."

"Will she give it?"

"I don't know," said Judy in a low voice.

"Now she's got married herself, what can *she* say?"

"She oughtn't to say anything!" exclaimed Judy, tilting her head. "But Mummy's got rather rigid ideas about marriage. She has never believed in short engagements, she used to say so. Nor what she calls 'rushing headlong into things.' You can see what she's like. It took her years to decide before she married Robert Tracy. And she's always said that she wouldn't want me to marry before I was at least twenty-one."

"Oh, well," said Elizabeth. "If she refused, you and Tony will have to be engaged and stick it."

Judy did not reply. But she thought of two days ago . . . Sunday. . . . She and Tony had gone on a bus down to Richmond Park, eaten a picnic lunch under the green trees, and sunbathed afterwards. They had been idiotically happy, found so much to laugh about and talk about, made so many marvelous plans . . . and built so many castles in the air. Just before they packed up their picnic to come home Tony had taken her in his arms for a moment and she had felt the deep passion of his hands and lips, and known that she was no longer a child . . . but all woman . . . eagerly responding to the ardour of the one and only man in the world. He had whispered against her hair:

"I couldn't bear waiting years. . . . I want you for my wife right now. I want to fight the world *with* you, not apart from you, my darling little Judy. Honestly, it would be the *end* if your mother refused her consent."

She could hear these words and feel his kiss upon her upturned mouth. She knew that she, too, could not bear to live apart from Tony for years. But there was still that awful bogy . . . she was under age. And Mummy *might* refuse. Not out of spite because Judy had been unsympathetic about *her*. No, Mummy wasn't like that, and Judy was the first to admit it; but because she might genuinely feel that it was wrong for Judy to rush into an immediate marriage in all the existing circumstances.

Judy felt a tremendous longing to win her mother over to her side. If she had been a more subtle character . . . more of a schemer . . . she might have decided there and then to rush down to Cooltye and coax her mother . . . *bribe* her with love and flattery into saying "yes." But Judy was not like that. She was too scrupulous—too straightforward. She could not pretend that she approved of Mummy's marrying Robert Tracy because *she* wanted something out of her.

No . . . she would just send that request for permission and pray for the best.

But as she posted the letter, and walked with Elizabeth down Draycott Avenue, Judy felt far from certain that everything was going to be easy. Depression seized her, which increased when Tony met her at the door of the maisonette and himself looked harassed and cross.

"The old man's still carrying on," he announced. "Says the question of our being able to afford to marry doesn't count as much as the fact that we're *both* too young and unsettled. And he keeps saying he had a settled job when *he* married Mamma—security and all that. He forgets that pre-war chaps could offer that kind of thing to a girl much more easily and that today we've got to fight for it together . . . and *that we don't mind*."

"Oh, Tony!" cried Judy, and shook her head dismally. Elizabeth said:

"Pop'll come round. It's just the first shock. Mamma won't be easy for a while, either. But we'll all talk things over after dinner. Don't let's mention it *during*. . . ."

Tony, with an arm round Judy's waist, leading her into the sitting-room, dropped a kiss on her head.

"Cheer up, sweetness," he whispered.

She took off her hat and shook back thick coppery hair from a hot, flushed young face.

"Even if we can convince *your* parents . . . we've got *my* mother to contend with and this ridiculous age business."

"You shouldn't be such an infant," he teased her, trying to snap out of his own depression. He was crazy about Judy, and quite determined to marry her in the face of all odds. He could bank on no financial help from home and would not dream of asking for it. He was as fully prepared as Judy to "manage" on their small combined incomes until he qualified and got a job. But on Judy's side it was different. It was illegal for her to marry without consent of her parents. Thinking of it in the plural, he said:

"I suppose we've got a step-papa to contend with as well as mother, down in Cooltye."

Judy went red, then positively white.

"It's nothing whatsoever to do with Uncle . . . I mean . . . Robert."

Tony chewed his lip.

"Nothing in theory . . . but he's your mamma's husband and he'll advise her. Who's side will he be on?"

"I couldn't care less," said Judy coldly.

Tony laughed and cupped her angry little face between his fine, slim fingers.

"I adore you when you look like that—little tiger-cat. You amuse me. So darned independent and strong-minded."

She tried to laugh and snuggled her cheek against his shoulder, sighing.

"It's all so fatuous. To have to *get* permission to marry you, my darling Tony."

"Well, Mrs. Green is really very sweet and quite romantic. . . . I'm sure she'll be sympathetic with us. If she refuses, I'll pop down and make her change her mind."

Judy tried to laugh and be gay with him. She knew that nobody could ever *make* Mummy do anything. Mummy had an extraordinary firm will and absolutely cast-iron principles under that gentle façade of hers. If she didn't approve of this marriage, if she really felt that it was a question of Judy being beguiled into it because of trouble at home, she would never give her consent . . . *never*.

And all through that evening—even though Mr. and Mrs. Chapman had at last drunk a toast to the engagement (marriage was not mentioned again), Judy travelled in her mind with her letter down to Cooltye and saw her mother opening it at the breakfast table tomorrow morning. *And after that . . . what?*

10

WHEN Katherine Tracy received that letter from Judy she was sitting in the big kitchen of Cooltye Farm at breakfast with Robert. He wore what he called his "working clothes," ready to go down on the farm with Armstrong. Sally sat at his side, golden eyes fixed on him with slavish devotion. Pip and Squeak were curled in their baskets in a corner, but they, too, kept watchful gaze upon the two humans *and* the Collie. (During the last three weeks these animals had learned to live together without fighting, but it was an armed truce and there were occasional setbacks with much bristling and snarling on all sides.)

Katherine was quite happy until the post came. It was once more glorious summer weather. The sun streamed goldenly into the big kitchen which she had grown to love, making the copper pans gleam on their shelves, and showing up the whiteness of the new paint.

They were still without living-in servants. The domestic situation was not as easy as they had imagined—or rather as Robert had hoped—because Katherine had not been so optimistic. Of the couples they had interviewed, either the man was good and the woman bad—or the reverse. They had now decided to engage a couple of Austrian girls, for whom they had to wait a month, and meanwhile Mrs. Askell was doing the rough work and Katherine the cooking. When Robert protested, Katherine assured him that she did not mind it. It was quite a change from pounding on a typewriter, she said, and she need not begin a children's book for her new contract until the autumn.

Certainly his wife looked well and happy, Robert thought tenderly, as he turned towards her and met her smiling gaze.

The last three weeks had seemed like a wonderful dream. Katherine fitted in so well as the mistress of Cooltye Farm and already had won Armstrong over completely. There was not a man or a land-girl on the farm today who would not do as much for Mrs. Tracy as for "the boss."

They had their friends who came to play a game of cards or have some music in the evenings. They drove into Brighton at weekends for some sea air—a theatre or a cinema. Katherine assured him that she was living a really "gay" life these days. She had become such a hermit with the children. She thoroughly enjoyed her freedom as Robert's wife, for freedom it was, and not by any means a new bondage. He continued to spoil her disgracefully.

Then came the bombshell of Judy's letter into the quiet kitchen. . . . Robert saw his wife's face flush as she read it. She stood up quickly and the colour ebbed from her face again, leaving her unusually pale. He saw her slim brown fingers brush the crumbs nervously from her lap, then smooth a crease in the fresh blue linen dress. He, too, rose to his feet.

"Have you had bad news, darling?"

Katherine, her heart thumping, handed him the letter.

"I knew it!" she said in a choked voice. "This is what I've dreaded all the way along."

Anxiously Robert scanned Judy's long scrawl. His first reaction was one of aggravation because once again young Judy was causing this beloved woman pain. But the next was a half-humorous sympathy for Judy. After all, the kid had her own life to make, and if she wanted to marry this chap, why not? He handed the letter back to Katherine and calmly lit his pipe.

"Well, darling, I don't see that it is such a tragedy."

"But it *is*, Rob!" she exclaimed, flushed again with deep emotional feeling. "It's just exactly what I didn't want . . . for Judy to rush headlong into marriage just because she has lost her own home and background. This was exactly what I always tried to tell you might result if I married again."

Robert puffed at his pipe, eying her over it.

"But, sweet, why should it be such a disaster? Isn't this Tony Chapman a nice fellow?"

Katherine spread out her hands, her brows knit together.

"Oh, he's all right. Actually I've only seen him once or twice. He came down to the cottage one weekend last summer. He's the brother of this girl with whom Judy works."

"Nice family and all that?"

"Yes, although I don't care for *Mrs.* Chapman. I haven't actually met her, but Judy described her as 'brass-haired and bridge mad'!"

Robert laughed.

"Sounds interesting as a mother-in-law for our Judy."

Katherine came round to him and looked earnestly into his smiling face.

"Don't joke, Rob. It's more serious than you think. Whatever the boy is like . . . and I am sure he's nice enough, and very good-looking as far as I remember . . . Judy must not get married now. She's only nineteen, and she's had absolutely no experience of men. Tony is her first affair. It would be madness."

He put an arm around her shoulder. He was growing accustomed to the warm, sensitive nature of the woman he had made his wife. When she loved, it was to the uttermost, and he could feel and respect the fierce mother-love in her desire to protect her "fledgling." He was not Judy's father. He fell to wondering what David Green would have thought about this thing. Somehow, from his own point of view, it did not seem too bad so long as the young man concerned was integral.

He asked a few more questions. There seemed nothing wrong with Tony Chapman except his youth and the fact that he was still a medical student. Katherine had even admitted that he had a little money of his own. Not much, but something, which helped in these hard times.

"Honestly, Kath," said Robert. "I don't think you should object to this marriage. Judy might do a lot worse."

Katherine looked up at him with brilliant eyes.

"But I'm not looking at it from that point of view, Rob! It would be all the same to me if Tony had £1,000 a year of his own. It is not so much that Judy is too young to know her own mind, but that nothing will make me believe it isn't just reaction after *what I have done.*"

Robert looked grave and a little uneasy.

"Darling, you're making rather an issue of your own marriage."

"No! No!" Katherine protested. "Judy made the issue when she walked out on me. Don't forget that she refused even to come to our wedding reception."

"But she did come to the wedding!" he reminded her with a whimsical smile.

"Oh, Rob, you're such a darling! Why the dickens should *you* be on Judy's side when she has been so hateful towards you?"

Now he laughed.

"I'll never really hold it against her. She was just at the age to be badly hit by the thought of her mother taking on a new husband. And we weren't seeing eye to eye before that. No . . . I'm not troubled about Judy's attitude to me. Only her behaviour towards *you*, my darling."

"Well, I've always been willing to forgive that," said Katherine in a low voice, "because I understand, too. But I'm not going to let her rush into this wedding. I don't think it's fair to *him or* Judy."

"These young people of today seem able to work things out in their own way. Look at my god-daughter, Amanda Jenkins . . . you remember my telling you about her. Ran away from home at seventeen to marry a penniless artist, and they've already got two babies, but seem perfectly happy and satisfied to rough it."

"I'll believe that!" said Katherine. "I'll believe that Judy might be happy roughing it with Tony. But only for a while. She has yet to mature. I wouldn't like to say what would happen to Amanda in a few years, either. I don't know her or why she ran away from home."

"Just a romantic elopement."

"There you are! So this is *different*. Judy has lost her own home and background. And that's *my* fault. I robbed her of them, so she is grabbing another kind."

Robert bit his lip and stared at the bowl of his pipe.

"Kath, darling, I'd hate to think that you were regret-ting——"

She broke in with passionate emphasis:

"No, no. Don't even suggest such a thing. I'd marry you over again, even if Pat went against me, as well as Judy. You know how much I love you, Rob."

He drew her close to his side for a moment, and there was such obvious honest relief in his eyes that she abandoned the subject of Judy for the moment and continued to reassure him of her love. Then when he released her she returned with a painful sigh to Judy's letter.

"She wants permission for an immediate wedding."

"Are his people willing?"

"I don't yet know. I shouldn't imagine they'll be pleased, but as Tony is over-age and can bring something to the exchequer, I suppose his people's consent isn't so important to him."

"Well, if I were you I'd let them get on with it, provided you really like the fellow," said Robert.

"But I don't *know* him. And Judy isn't grown up . . . she's still my baby . . ." Katherine broke off, and now there were tears in her eyes. She felt horribly miserable and anxious for Judy. Nothing that Robert could say alleviated her fears or could make her believe that Judy was not merely taking on Tony and matrimony as the least line of resistance . . . a way out . . . something a bit better than her lonely "digs." She had missed her home life, naturally, poor darling. Tony offered love and companionship. She was fascinated by him (although it was hard for Katherine to connect little Judy with passionate love). But she knew she had to get used to that idea sooner or later, though she *could not* agree with Robert that it was a good thing for Judy to rush headlong into marriage. She *must* have time to think it well out and see a great deal more of Tony first.

"You must forgive me, and try to understand, darling, if I feel very strongly about this," at length Katherine said to her husband. "But it would be against my every instinct to say 'yes.' I shall ask Judy to become formally engaged . . . we'll put it in the papers . . . we'll entertain Tony, and I'll go and see his people, and so on. But a rush marriage I can not and will not agree to while Judy is so young."

Robert said:

"You're her mother, sweet, and I must bow to your superior judgment."

"Don't you see what I'm driving at?" she asked, anxious to feel that he was in accordance with her over this, as in everything else.

"I understand your anxiety, and she *is* only nineteen. But——"

"Oh, Rob!" she interrupted. "It isn't even as if I could be sure of Tony—whether he'd take care of her properly. I must get to know him a bit. I simply never thought of him as a possible husband for Judy when he came down to the cottage. She seemed to me then hardly more than a schoolgirl."

Robert gave a humorous smile.

"I've always heard that mothers find it hard to realize it when their ewe lambs have grown into sensible young sheep."

She tried to laugh with him.

"So speaks the farmer! And sheep are *never* sensible!"

He passed a hand caressingly over her fair head. He could feel that she was still deeply distressed. Above all things he wanted her to be happy, his Katherine, who had fought so long and bravely for her children. He said:

"Think it over, darling, and we'll discuss it again during lunch. I must push off now. I'm expecting the vet at half past nine. You know we've got old Mayblossom sick, and she's one of my best Jerseys. . . ."

Then he was gone. Katherine was left alone to worry and fret all that morning while she worked around the house. She did, however, mention Judy's letter to the faithful Mrs. Askell, who had known them all so many years. Mrs. Askell was on her side at once.

"I don't hold with young girls marrying before twenty-one. They don't know their own minds, and Miss Judy's younger than most for her age."

Katherine hugged this agreement to herself. And the more she thought about it, the more she believed, deep down within her, that not only was Judy too young, but too prejudiced by recent events.

At lunch-time she told Robert that she had decided to write to Judy and suggest a year's engagement.

But Judy was not waiting for the reply. She put a call through to Cooltye Farm that same night.

"Well, Mummy, did you get my letter?" asked her anxious young voice.

As soon as Katherine heard that dear and familiar voice her knees began to shake a little. She did so hate fighting with her children, and this was bound to be a battle. Besides, she longed to get Judy back rather than drive her yet farther away. But Judy had been right about her mother's cast-iron principles. And Katherine was as straightforward and scrupulous as her daughter. She would not concede a point just to make herself popular. She told Judy quietly but definitely that she could not give her the permission for which she asked.

Judy started off by showing bitter disappointment. She shot a volley of "whys" down the telephone, to all of which Katherine repeated the explanation that she did not want Judy to rush into marriage without giving it serious thought.

"Let us announce the engagement and leave it like that for the moment, darling, please," she ended.

Then Judy became furiously indignant.

"You have no right to try and order my life about. You've settled your own. *You've* got married . . . why shouldn't I?"

Katherine, sitting at Robert's desk, white as a sheet and trembling now, said:

"That is exactly what I am trying to point out to you. You're only doing this because *I've* chosen to get married again. The whole thing is a kind of rebound from *my* affair, and I'm not going to let you do it. Any other mother would feel the same. Even if you were over twenty-one, I would suggest a proper engagement."

There followed a storm from Judy, punctuated by the "pips" every three minutes. It was typical of Katherine then that she should remember Judy's slender means and say:

"I think we'd better reverse this call, Judy darling. . . ."

When the reverse had been put through, Tony came on to the line. Judy was telephoning from his home.

He was less passionate and more controlled than Judy. In a winning voice he tried to beguile Katherine.

"Honestly Mrs. . . . er . . . Tracy—you can't think how

much I shall love having you for a mother-in-law. You've always been one of my 'pin-up girls', you know."

Katherine tried to laugh, but she was adamant.

"Don't flatter me, Tony. I think you're very sweet and I shall like having *you* for a son-in-law, too. But I wish you and Judy wouldn't rush things. You know that she's been upset because I got married again, and——"

"But it's not that which made her decide to marry me," Tony broke in. "We've fallen in love. Even if you were still at the Thatched Cottage as in the old days, I think Judy would still have wanted to marry me."

"I'm afraid that is what I doubt," said Katherine. "I think the old Judy would have been quite willing to stay home and have an engagement."

Here Judy took over the telephone again.

"That may be, Mummy, but as I haven't *got* a home, and as I'm alone in London, I don't see why I shouldn't be allowed to join forces with Tony."

Before the words were out she realized that she had only convicted herself in her mother's eyes. Gently, but firmly, Katherine persisted in her refusal. And then Judy burst into angry tears. She sobbed down the wires:

"I think its monstrous of you, Mummy . . . you've got the whip-hand, just because I'm only nineteen . . . it isn't fair . . . you'll make me *hate* you——"

She broke off, choking. Katherine, ice-cold and deeply distressed, heard Tony say:

"Take it easy, my sweet. This isn't getting us anywhere. . . ."

Tony came on the telephone again. Katherine said in an anguished voice:

"Oh, Tony, please try and make Judy understand that I'm not just trying to hurt her. It will break my heart if this merely drives us farther apart. I suppose it would all be easy if I just said 'yes,' but I can't, when it's so plain to me that Judy is rushing into this because she doesn't care for my husband, and won't live here at Cooltye Farm. Tony, I can't *bear* it if she hates me. . . ." Her own voice broke. But she added: "Try to make her understand. Come down here, both of you, and see me, please. Try to look at things from my point of view. Judy is only nineteen. Wait a year . . . surely that isn't too much to ask!"

"Well, it's a bit long when you're so much in love," came from Tony, with a deep laugh. "I do hope you'll change your mind. Judy's in a terrible state; she's crying her eyes out. . . ."

Katherine felt torn in two. Her hand shook so that she could scarcely hold the telephone. The tears were pouring down her own cheeks now. (Thank goodness Rob wasn't here to witness this—he had been called out again to that valuable Jersey that was so ill.)

The telephone call ended without satisfaction for either side. Katherine, after she had put the instrument down on its rest, leaned her head on her folded arms and cried . . . even as she knew that her young daughter was crying, up there in London. Was she doing wrong in withholding her permission to that marriage? *Was* she? It was so hard to go on being ruthless when she knew that those two young things were so much in love . . . and yet . . . how could she ever convince herself that it was *love alone* which urged Judy into this lightning marriage? She could hear the echo of that passionate young voice, *"You'll make me hate you."*

Of course, Judy had lost her temper. She didn't mean that. She could never hate her own mother. But Katherine could see that tonight's conversation had been disastrous . . . had widened the branch between her daughter and herself. And it *did* seem mean of her to withhold from Judy the kind of happiness which she, her mother, had just taken for herself in full.

For the rest of that evening, until Robert returned, Katherine worried and argued with herself.

She even wrote another letter to Judy, begging her to try and see things sensibly and agree to an engagement.

"Don't hate me, darling, please. Try to look at things from my point of view. I am trying to do my duty, and not to cull favour with you or Tony. But I do so want us all to be friends. Bring Tony down here, please, and send me his full name, etc., so that I can put the engagement in The Times *and* Telegraph *for you. . . ."*

She said nothing to Robert about that fatal telephone conversation. He was looking very tired when he came in, and upset because all the work had not been able to save Mayblossom's life. And the life of a valuable Jersey cow means much to a farmer—apart from the sense of failure, after hours of struggle down there in the shed. Katherine, by this time, was, herself, more composed. She made a strong cup of tea for Robert and then sat quietly with him listening to his troubles. She had no right to inflict her own upon him at a time like this, she thought. He had been listening to the Judy problem all day. This evening she must remember that she was the farmer's wife as well as Judy's mother.

But while Robert slept, exhausted, Katherine lay awake worrying about Judy. She, like Robert, wondered what David would have done, and then reminded herself ironically that had David lived the situation would never have arisen, for Judy would never have left home. So once again the cycle of her thoughts came round to the original conclusion . . . which was that Judy had rushed from her arms into Tony's, and that it would be absolutely wrong for her, Katherine, to let the girl tie herself up to Tony Chapman without due consideration.

The following week Pat came home on his leave, having met Judy in town on his way down to Cooltye.

Katherine had the usual warm welcome waiting for her soldier son, and knowing him well—how he hated too much formality—she did not get out the best silver or china. She laid his tea on the kitchen table. A pot of strong tea, plenty of scones, farm butter and honey and one of her own chocolate cakes, which he adored.

"I say, Mum, this is terrific!" he exclaimed, as soon as he had changed out of that unbecoming khaki and come down to the meal. He looked admiringly round the big homely kitchen.

"Robert's out this afternoon," said his mother, and her eyes glowed as she looked at him. He was bronzed and fit after his session up at Languard Fort. She could even see the hint of a tiny moustache on his upper lip. She didn't know whether to laugh or cry at the sight of it. Her Pat, with a moustache! A man, indeed! They sat down together. Everything seemed like it used to be at the cottage . . . free and easy and friendly, with both of them laughing and chatting. Pat said how well *she* looked, and congratulated her on the change in the farmhouse.

"It's all looking lovely, Mum. . . ."

Then the name of Judy arose, and immediately Katherine felt a cold curtain fall between her son and herself. For Pat, nervously lowering those long lashes of his, bluntly declared that he was entirely on his sister's side.

"Tony's a decent chap. I've seen them both. I can't see why you're against it, Mum," he said.

She brought out all the arguments which she had given to Robert.

"Can't you see, Pat, that she's only refusing to have an ordinary engagement because . . . well, because of the rift between us? Normally she would have lived at home and been glad to wait until Tony qualified."

Pat pulled out a packet of cigarettes from his pocket and tapped one thoughtfully on the box.

"Yep . . . but don't forget, things aren't quite normal or as they used to be, Mum."

All the happiness fled from Katherine's eyes.

"Oh, why must you both feel that anything has changed, when I still love you both so much!" she cried in a heartbroken voice.

Pat lit his cigarette, his cheeks hot.

"We love you, too, Mum but——"

"You do, but Judy doesn't," she broke in.

"She does at heart, but you don't quite understand her attitude of mind."

"And you do?"

"Yes. From her point of view, she has lost you to Robert, and nice as this home is, it isn't really *hers* any more. Tony is offering her one of her own, and with him in it. That's O.K. Let them get on with it, that's what I say."

Katherine stood up and walked to the windows. The sun was shining. The round pond was a mirror of silver light. The oak trees looked gloriously green, and the gladioli, which were Robert's favourite flowers, and especially good this year, made a vivid splash of scarlet along the borders. But the pleasant scene was all blurred by her tears. She said:

"You none of you seem to *understand* why I refuse my permission. And it's no good going over it all again. But I just *know* that I'm doing right, even if you all think me hard. Judy *must* have time in which to think things out, and I will not let her rush into marriage because I have married again."

Pat looked at his mother's determined back. He knew that determination. He admired her for it. He admired anybody who had the courage of their convictions. And in his mind there was nobody in the world like Mum. Be he felt sorry for Judy when he saw her this morning. She had seemed quite *changed* from the jolly "kid sister" of the past. Poor old Snub Nose—looking so much older. She had lost her healthy colour. She had assured him that working in the shop suited her, but that it was their mother's refusal to let her get married that was making her ill. When he had asked her about Tony's people, she had said that they preferred Tony to wait until he was qualified, but weren't going to tell him "never to darken their doors again" or any nonsense of that sort. No, Mummy was the only barrier to her happiness.

"Ju is absolutely sure that she wants to marry this chap," Pat suddenly said aloud to his mother.

Katherine swung round, her chin tilted.

"Then she can wait like other girls have waited, and let him get his degree and give her a proper home. By that time *she* will be quite sure, and *I* shan't be afraid that she had just been driven into it."

Pat ran his fingers through his thick hair.

"Well, it's your show and not mine, Mum. Let's quit talking about it," he said. "Only I thought I'd let you know that Ju's pretty miserable."

Those words seemed to cut Katherine to the heart, and once again she felt how easy it would be for her to give in and have them all rushing to her telling her what an angel she was! But she refused to do it.

They said no more about Judy, but even Pat's homecoming had been spoiled for Katherine. If Ju was miserable, how much more miserable was *she*, who was in the first instance responsible for all this upheaval!

After Pat had gone to bed, Robert stole a glance at his wife's face. He had said nothing, but he had noticed all the evening how quiet and depressed she seemed. He said:

"Everything all right with the lad?"

"Oh, fine. He's getting on so well, and seems more at home in the Army now."

"He's a darned nice chap, your son, Kath. I don't think I mentioned it to you, did I, but I'm seeing old Grover, my lawyer, next Monday. I've decided to change my will—to leave some of my money to your Pat. He might even take a fancy to the farming side once he's done his service."

Katherine, who had felt wretched ever since the conversation with Pat, lifted a flushed face and grateful eyes to her husband.

"That's more than good of you, Rob."

He added:

"Not forgetting Judy, the young rascal . . . she must have her bit."

Then Katherine burst into tears, which was so unlike her that Robert was frankly alarmed. His practical, courageous Katherine crying! He gathered her in his arms, and questioned and comforted her. And after he had listened to all that she had to say, he had an idea.

"Look here. You know I've got to go up to town for the National Farmers' Conference on Friday? I'll pop into that flower shop and take young Judy out for some lunch. I'll make her come, whether she wants to or not. And I'll suggest she gets hold of her medical student and we'll all talk this over."

Katherine, drying her eyes, ashamed of her weakness, whispered:

"You're too good to me, Rob. What do you mean to say?"

"Just have a chat and see what the boy is like, too. After all, I used to have to 'vet' a lot of young fellows when I was in the Navy. I'm a fairly good judge of character."

Katherine put her arms round his neck and hugged him close to her.

"You're the best husband in the whole world, and the most understanding!" she said.

"I only want you to be happy, Katherine, and I know you never will be wholly so until this Judy business is cleared up," he said.

She did not answer. But she knew that he was right.

11

JUDY was not in a particularly good mood on that Friday of
the National Farmers' Conference. To begin with, there was
thunder in the air and the atmosphere in *Fleurette* seemed
rather like that of a steam-heated conservatory. Even Elizabeth, who didn't mind how it was, complained. But Judy
had a headache. She drooped in hothouse atmospheres. She
was too used to the country. Her thoughts continually turned
to Cooltye and this time last summer. But every time she
thought of it it was only to feel increasing resentment against
the man who had "taken Mummy away" from her. She had
also felt particularly unhappy when she heard that the
Thatched Cottage had been sold to "nice people" with children. It was hateful to her to think of even the nicest
strangers in her old home, of other children enjoying her
darling little bedroom (or picking apples off the trees in the
autumn, or the roses Mummy had planted so many years
ago). Childish and stupid, of course; she constantly re-
proached herself, but she couldn't "snap out of it"—not
even to please darling Tony, who was more philosophic (and,
of course, less personally upset by this metamorphosis in her
life).

Her engagement to Tony was, of course, a great tonic, and
she was madly happy when she was with him. But he was
working under terrific pressure in the hospital at the moment
and there were many evenings when they could not meet,
which gave her a lot of time in which to think and feel apprehensive. And to wish that Mummy was down at the
cottage *by herself*.

But Judy wouldn't go down to Cooltye Farm. She *wouldn't*.
It was a black day! Last night she had had rather a

wretched dinner with the Chapmans, too. Mrs. Chapman was now "doing her duty"—had acknowledged her as Tony's future wife—and was "resigned," as she put it, to this wedding at the end of August. But neither she nor Mr. Chapman really approved. Dear Elizabeth was the only one who had come round and was giving them wholehearted support.

While Judy forced herself out of her langour on this hot morning, and sold flowers to difficult customers who complained not only of the weather, but the prices, she remembered last night uncomfortably.

Tony had been sitting beside her at the table and surreptitiously taken her hand, which had comforted her while he announced cheerfully that he and Judy were "looking for suitable digs." Mr. Chapman had grunted, "hope you find them" and Mrs. Chapman, with claws showing through the velvet gloves, smiled sweetly at Judy and said:

"It doesn't do for young couples to live with their in-laws, otherwise I'd have you both here. But I *do* think it is a pity that you've got to rough it, you poor dears, especially while darling Tony is working so hard and needs the good meals he is used to at home."

Judy had flushed and kept silent. Tony had laughed and said:

"I bet Judy will feed me like a king."

Mrs. Chapman, still with that acid smile, said:

"Does dear Judy know much about cooking? Didn't your mother do most of it in your home, dear?"

Yes, it had been *that* sort of evening. And Judy had gone home feeling that the world was against her—trying to make things seem as difficult as possible for Tony and herself. But it had only served to make her more than ever determined to go through with the fight. That was the stuff Judy was made of.

When Robert Tracy walked into the little florist's at about half past twelve Judy was so astonished she almost dropped the bunch of carnations which she was in process of arranging.

He approached her, smiling, taking off his hat. He was an unfamiliar Robert in his dark town suit, carrying a rolled umbrella. She had to admit he looked rather smart, and particularly brown and well. But even as she met his friendly smile she stiffened in every limb.

"Hullo," she said with an unconcern she was far from feeling. "What are *you* doing up here?"

"Up on a conference," he said. "How are you, Judy?"

"I'm fine, thanks, Unc—Robert," she corrected herself. Personally Robert thought that she looked rather seedy, thinner, older-looking, rather pathetic, really. He said, very kindly:

"I want to talk to you, my dear, so thought I would take you out for a spot of lunch if you'd like to come."

Her lashes drooped. She looked nervously at the flowers which she started to arrange in a tall vase.

"Awfully nice of you, but actually, when Elizabeth comes back from her lunch, I'm meeting Tony Chapman—he's my fiancé."

"That's splendid," said Robert. "You can both lunch with me. Nothing could be better. I haven't yet had the pleasure of meeting Tony."

Judy felt cornered. She found it difficult to snap out of her black mood, and she had looked forward to seeing Tony alone because he could not meet her tonight. The last person she wanted as a "third" was Mummy's husband. (Those last two words made her squirm as she said them to herself. *Mummy's husband.*) But Robert was making it difficult for her because he was being so awfully nice. He took the wind out of her sails.

"If I won't be in the way with you two young things, I'd very much like you both to lunch at my club. I'll ring up from here and order a table."

"We only get an hour off . . ." stammered Judy.

"Then we'll find a place somewhere up here, near your shop. Didn't I see a Grill just across the road near Harrods?"

"Yes. We never go there. It's too expensive."

Robert smiled. He could see how the girl still felt about him. Unfriendly . . . unrelenting. Poor old Judy! Yet he was not conscious of resentment nor even of the faintest malice. She was Katherine's daughter and there was something in the contours of that young face, now that it was so much thinner, reminiscent of Katherine. It made him feel tenderly toward Judy—anxious for his own sake as well as Katherine's to bridge the gulf.

"Where were you meeting your young man?" he asked.

"In our usual bun shop," she said dryly.

"Right, then we'll pick him up there and go over to the Grill."

She could not refuse. Now she listened, without letting him see how hungry she was for news, to all that he had to tell her about her mother. He had seated himself in the chair which she had coldly but politely offered him, and was lighting a cigarette.

She eagerly drank in the news of Cooltye, glad to know that her mother was well and to hear all about Pip and Squeak. She had missed the darling Corgis. Yet, charming as Robert was being, she could not stop resenting him. Wasn't *he* responsible for her loss, her home-sickness? All very well for him to sit here and smile. He was her *stepfather*. And that was a grim thought to Judy.

At one o'clock she locked up the shop and walked round the corner beside Robert. He thought that she looked charming in her yellow and white checked cotton dress and white sandals, with white nylon bag slung over her shoulder—her coppery curls bare. She might be that same light-hearted child whom he had seen growing up in Cooltye. The real change in Judy was mental rather than physical, Robert reflected. It was sad that he should be the primary cause of her unhappiness. Yet when he questioned her about her engagement she cheered up and spoke with enthusiasm; she seemed sincerely devoted to her young man. Not merely infatuated, as Katherine had feared. Tony was wonderful, she said, and going a long way in his profession. When Robert suggested that they might have a fight to make ends meet, she said:

"I couldn't care less. As long as we're together, what does it matter? If you've got enough to eat and a roof over your head, money isn't all that important."

If she expected antagonism from "Mummy's husband" over this she was surprised. He agreed with her. Money *wasn't* everything, he said. But a little of it, and some security, was essential. Romance was fine until one found oneself hungry or homeless, he added with a laugh. Judy conceded this, then added:

"At Tony's and my age we don't expect so much of the comforts and luxuries as the older people."

She was supported in this argument by Tony, after the three of them had met and were settled at their table, eating their lunch.

Tony had been surprised to find Judy with her stepfather, but not displeased. It was quite a good thing for him to make Robert Tracy's acquaintance, as he told Judy afterwards, and he was as agreeably astonished as Judy when Katherine's husband seemed more on their side than *hers*.

Robert ordered them a lunch which was more than satisfying, and a large beer for Tony. He said:

"I approve of young marriages so long as the two people concerned aren't rushing blindly into it. What I mean to say is that the primary *motive* for marriage is the most important thing."

Judy and Tony exchanged glances. Tony, enjoying his meal said:

"Well, I think our motive is a pretty normal one. We are just very much in love with each other, sir."

Robert wiped his lips with his table-napkin, sat back and looked at his young guests. They did seem so *very* young. Yet they were in love . . . obviously so, with all the fire and fervour of their youth. And he had to admit that he liked the look of this young medical student with his keen, intelligent face. He had nice manners, too. Youngsters today behaved rather casually towards each other . . . there was a lot of affectionate teasing and leg-pulling and nothing that could be called Victorian "treacle" . . . or false sentiment. They spoke openly about everything . . . even the facts of life. Tony declared calmly that they had no intention of having children until he had qualified and could put Judy in a proper home of her own.

Well, that all seemed to the good. Robert talked and listened. And the more he listened, the more he liked Judy's choice.

"But to return to this motive for marriage," he said.

"What I think your mother fears, Judy, is that you are rushing things because of the change down in Cooltye."

Judy looked quickly at Tony and then, with burning cheeks, at Robert Tracy. So he wanted her to come into the open and cross swords, did he? Well, she was quite willing.

"Whatever the situation was in Cooltye, Tony and I would still have wanted to get married, wouldn't we, Tony?"

"Yes, I think we would," the boy nodded. "It just happens that we didn't discover how much we wanted to be together until Judy was on her own."

"Ah!" said Robert thoughtfully.

Judy flashed:

"Oh, I dare say Mummy's marriage *has* had some bearing on it. But that doesn't mean Tony and I aren't sincerely in love, does it?"

Robert lifted his brows.

"No, it doesn't. But be sure about it."

"Whatever my motives are, I don't think Mummy has any right to withhold her permission!" exclaimed Judy.

Now Robert gave her a grave smile.

"My dear, she has every right. . . ."

"Well, I call it taking an unfair advantage of her power over me just because I'm a minor!" broke in Judy hotly, and her brilliant eyes sought Tony's support. He gave it quickly.

"I do think, sir, if you don't mind my saying so, that it's a little hard that parents should still be able to enforce this prehistoric law. In these days we grow up rather more quickly than you did. I *assure* you Judy knows her own mind."

"She's lucky. I wonder how many of us do," said Robert humorously.

"Well, I admit I'm not so slow to make up mine as Mummy is," said Judy.

Again Robert's brows went up.

"Well," at length he said, "although your mother is slower to act, Judy, she rarely makes mistakes. I know you can't get used to the idea, but we *are* very happy, and very glad we waited before making our decision to join forces."

Judy's lashes flickered. There was a dangerous glint in her eyes.

"Which is awfully nice for you both, but how about *us*? Must we be prevented from being happy just because Mummy has all kinds of unnecessary fears and inhibitions about *motives*?"

Robert signalled to a passing waiter to bring more beer for Tony. He could still sense the hostility in Katherine's daughter, but was still unmoved by it. It behooved him to be patient, he reflected. After all, he *had* in a measure taken away her mother and her old home. He said:

"Try to see things from your mother's point of view, Judy. All she wants is your well-being; your happiness."

"Then she shouldn't try and stop me from marrying Tony!" cried Judy.

Tony, with a sidelong glance at his fiancée, thought:

"What a darling she is! I adore her independent spirit. She could easily crawl to this chap. He isn't too much against us. But Judy will never crawl to anyone. And she's fiercely proud and loyal. She'll be like that in our marriage . . . bless her!"

Now Robert astonished Judy a little further.

"I'm inclined to agree with you, Judy," he said quietly. "Believe it or not as you like, my dear girl, I'm on your side about this."

It flashed across Judy's mind:

"Perhaps he just wants to get rid of me once and for all. . . ."

Then she dismissed this reaction as unworthy. Robert, if nothing else, was honest and decent. And as she listened to him talk for the next ten minutes she felt a queer reluctant admiration for him stealing over her. He seemed to see things from young people's point of view even better than Mummy. Much better, in fact, since he was not *anti* their immediate marriage.

"You've both got plenty of pluck, and Tony is obviously going to get on like a house on fire when he qualifies. . . . I don't think it would matter much if you did have to struggle at first. I think even your mother may reach that decision once she is sure that her own recent actions haven't driven you to the altar, so to speak."

He gave Judy his kindly, humorous smile again.

Now she met his gaze with a tinge of gratitude in her own.

"Well, I must say I'd be awfully grateful if you could make Mummy agree with you."

His smile broadened.

"It isn't my policy to try and *make* your delightful mother do anything, my dear Judy."

"Well, I expect you've got plenty of influence over her," said Judy, with a bitterness which Robert discreetly ignored.

"I say, sir, it really would be terrific if you could persuade Mrs. . . . er . . . Tracy," Tony stammered, "to give us the okay."

"Well, I suggest you both come down to the Farm this weekend and we'll have a family conference," said Robert.

Tony was swift to accept the invitation.

"I think it would be a fine idea, sir, and a weekend in the country would do Judy good."

The girl sat back, silent. Her heart beat a trifle fast with the new thrilling hope that her mother might indeed be persuaded to permit her to get married at once. At the same time she felt uneasy. This all savoured too much of complete capitulation and surrender to Robert Tracy. It was not easy for one of Judy's deep and rather complex nature to drift with the tide . . . alter her likes and dislikes or overcome her prejudices quickly. Even as a child she could never be wooed by strangers or sycophants with bribes or flattery. She was not going to allow herself to be bribed by Robert Tracy now, even though he seemed anxious to help her and Tony. He was the original cause of the trouble and should not be allowed to forget it. At the same time, she had to admit it would be rather exciting to go down to Cooltye and see Mummy and get her permission. She looked at Tony. He smiled back into her eyes—his own bright with hope. Then Judy turned to her stepfather.

"Well, thanks very much," she said awkwardly. "It would be jolly decent of you if you would say a word on our behalf."

"It shall be done," he said. "And now I must get the bill and fly. I'm catching an early train back. Can't stand London in this weather, and you two will be late for your jobs."

He left them together outside the Grill and hopped on to a bus. Judy looked at her fiancé. He said:

"There's thunder in the air, and I think we're going to have the devil of a storm, and I'm livid because I can't take you out tonight, angel. But none of that matters if we can get the okay from your mother."

"No, nothing matters but that," she breathed, and hugged his arm to her side. "Oh, Tony, Tony . . . wouldn't it be wonderful?"

"I think that Step-papa is a damn' nice chap," added Tony. "Couldn't have been more friendly towards us, could he?"

Grudgingly, Judy admitted this to be so. But after Tony had gone and she walked back to *Fleurette* she faced what she thought a rather "ghastly possibility"; that she might have to owe her future happiness to her old enemy . . . and the one thing she had never wanted was to be under any obligation to *him*. She felt a conflict of emotions . . . all tied up in herself. One day, she supposed, it would straighten itself out. Meanwhile there was rather a lot to go through. *And would Mummy lift the "ban" even if Robert advised her to do so?*

Judy was still harassed, full of doubts and confusions as she returned to work. And not a little nervous when she remembered that she had conceded so far as to promise Robert that she would take Tony down to Cooltye Farm this weekend.

12

FOR the second time Robert told his Katherine exactly what had transpired between Judy, Tony and himself.

She sat on a stool at his feet with the two Corgis spread out on the rug in front of her and Sally lying behind Robert's chair, a trifle sulkily. Robert's arm was round his wife's shoulders. Darkness had fallen, the lamps were alight, and it looked cosy and attractive in the sitting-room of Cooltye Farm. And Katherine looked the most attractive thing in it, her husband told her, and smiled as she made him repeat again everything that they had said during lunch: what Judy had been wearing; all the details which a woman likes to know and which a man finds hard to remember.

Then, having taken it all in, Katherine laced slim brown hands over hunched knees, shook her head and sighed.

"Just imagine! Those two lunching with you. . . . I feel almost jealous. It seems such *years* since I had even a few moments alone with my daughter."

"Well, I hope you'll get more than that this weekend."

"You think they *will* come down?" Katherine asked anxiously.

"They said they would. The young man, in my opinion, is an extraordinarily nice chap. Naturally, he isn't as het up about *us* as Judy, so is inclined to be more tolerant. I think he will influence Judy for the best."

Katherine turned shining, earnest eyes upon her husband.

"You've been wonderful, Rob, and it was more than good of you to take all that trouble. I only hope Judy realizes how you put yourself out for her."

He threaded his fingers through her hair, gently, marvelling at its silken texture. He loved the soft grey interwoven with the honey colour. He said:

"It was for you, even more than the child."

She caught his hand and pressed it against her cheek with that shy passion which made her so inexpressively dear to him—because there was something so eternally youthful about Katherine in such moods.

"Rob, you're an angel, but I am still very reluctant to let Judy have her own way. I'm relieved to know that Tony has passed his examination so far as *you* were concerned, but there is still this question of an *immediate* marriage. Didn't you ask them to wait?"

"I'm afraid I didn't," said Robert a trifle guiltily.

"But why——" she began.

"Dearest," he interrupted. "I honestly think that you should try not to interfere between those two. No matter how anxious you are about motives or their future, let them get on with it is my advice."

Katherine drew a deep breath.

"Oh, Rob, is it *really*?"

He nodded.

"Yes. If you try and enforce your right to stop their marriage you'll make Judy more defiant than ever and possibly antagonize her for good and all. It may even lead her to do something silly——" he broke off with a gesture.

"Oh, Rob, that's the last thing I want!" cried Katherine. "And you know what it means to me to have this misunderstanding with Judy. It's been *wretched*. I want so terribly to be friends with her again."

"Then let them get on with it," Robert said again. "Judy is a good kid at heart. Young Chapman will look after her, and if they have to pinch and scrape it won't do 'em any harm. They were right, you know, Kath, when they told me yesterday that they don't need the luxuries or security that we ask for at our age. They are content to take risks. Youth must find its own way and fight its own battles *and* find its own happiness. That's how I look at it, and that's why I'm sympathetic with them."

Katherine looked down at the strong hand which she was holding. It was so very strong and a little rough, and mahogany brown. The hand of a farmer; but with those long, sensitive fingers which were so tender, despite their hardness. When she looked up at his face again her eyes glittered with unshed tears.

"You're really a very grand person, Rob," she whispered, "and much *bigger* than I could ever hope to be."

He gave an embarrassed laugh, leaned forward and gathered her into his arms.

"Nonsense, sweet. There never lived a 'bigger' person than my Kath. But you're a woman, and emotional. Also, there's a very close tie between you and Judy and you've been very close together always, which puts things a bit out of perspective for you both. When you looked at me just now, it was so like your young Judy—half defiant and half afraid and too sweet for words . . . yes, you're sweet . . . the pair of you. . . ." He laughed again and hugged her.

She gave a long sigh and kissed him.

"We'll see what happens when they come down," she said; "and now it's time my farmer was in bed."

"Up with the lark," Robert laughed again. "Come on, Sally . . . come on you, Pip—Squeak—walkies . . . out you go!"

He walked into the hall and opened the front door. The three dogs rushed out with a mad scramble, snarling and barking and menacing any possible unseen stranger who might be lurking in the summer darkness.

Katherine began to switch off the lights. She felt happier but a little apprehensive at the prospect of the weekend and of how things would be between Judy and herself.

She did not really believe that Judy would come until she was actually there . . . Judy-like, having turned up without warning late on the Saturday afternoon, and having taken a bus from Hassocks Station down to the Spread Eagle.

"We didn't know when Tony would get away from the hospital, so we couldn't let you know in time to meet us," Judy explained.

Robert was out. Katherine was in the kitchen. She had just made a cherry cake and some scones. She had not even had time to take off her overall—when Judy and Tony knocked on the front door.

The mother's heart beat fast with joy and a touch of embarrassment as she looked at the daughter who had been away from her for so long, and at the tall, good-looking young man in grey flannels who stood beside her. (She had forgotten how handsome Tony was. No wonder he had captured her Judy!)

Her first impression about the girl was, as Robert's had been, that Judy was thinner and much older-looking, unaccustomedly neat and town-like in her tailored suit and straw hat.

Mother and daughter eyed each other. The next moment Katherine held out her arms and Judy was in them.

"Oh, darling!" exclaimed Katherine. "How *lovely* to see you!"

Judy allowed herself to be kissed, and kissed her mother back with real warmth. She had missed Katherine more than she could ever admit. And she had to admit, too, that she had never seen her mother look better . . . absurdly young, and beautiful, too.

"Gosh, it's hot!" she said, for something to say, as she disengaged herself from Katherine's embrace.

"A corking day to be in the country," put in Tony. "How *are* you, Mrs. Green . . . Tracy . . ." he coloured and added with a laugh, "I shall never remember."

Katherine coloured, too.

"Sometimes I wonder if I shall, Tony. Such a thing is habit and custom."

The next moment they were all in the kitchen. Judy threw off her coat and hat. Whilst they all chattered about nothing in particular her eyes roamed critically around, and found nothing but satisfaction in the sight of the cheerful kitchen with its real farmhouse atmosphere. Tea was spread on the table in the homeliest fashion. A huge bowl of marigolds burned a brilliant orange in the sunlight which slanted through the open window. Everything, as Judy had noted, walking through the house, bore marks now of her mother's personality. The fresh chintzes, exquisitely arranged flowers, books and pictures. Some of them familiar . . . this piece of furniture and that out of her old home. Oh yes, it could be called "coming home," walking into Cooltye Farm. She was not a stranger to the place, anyhow, for when they were small she and Pat used to come over here regularly to see "Uncle Robert" and have the fun of watching the cows being milked, or the butter churned in the dairy.

But after a moment Judy's first real pleasurable thrill in being down here with her mother again and of exchanging her unattractive "bed-sit" for the beauty of Cooltye Farm faded. She grew quiet and let Tony and her mother do most of the talking. Tony handed her a lighted cigarette. She put it between her lips and for an instant met his gay, warm gaze and answered it. Katherine unwittingly intercepted that gaze, and it gave her almost a shock. There was something so passionate and purposeful in it. It woke her up to the full realization that the nineteen-year-old Judy was no longer a schoolgirl, but a *woman* deeply in love. As deeply, pondered Katherine, as *she* loved her Robert. Heavens! How difficult for any mother to realize such a change and development had taken place in a daughter who seemed a short time ago to be a curly-headed rascal climbing the trees at the Thatched Cottage!

They none of them touched on personal matters until later on. All three of them seemed to shirk it—particularly Judy, who grew more nervous as time went on, and hung rather defiantly on Tony's arm as Katherine showed them round the house. Tony expressed wholehearted admiration. He had never, he said, seen such a perfect example of Jacobean architecture. What magnificent beams and floors! What an enchanting fireplace in the sitting-room with its high mantelpiece! Cooltye Farm combined beauty with all that was practical and "cosy" he said.

"Don't you adore it, darling?" he asked Judy.

Katherine seemed to hang on her daughter's reply. Judy said:

"I think it's absolutely perfect."

But the mother, with unerring instinct, knew what lay behind that quiet phrase.

Could Judy have been absolutely honest in this moment she would have added:

"*But I preferred our humble little cottage.*"

"*She will never forgive me,*" thought the mother, "*for taking away her own home.*"

There seemed nothing left for Katherine to do but to give Judy the opportunity to make a new home which would also be her own. And that meant stepping aside and watching her take on the responsibilities of marriage before she was twenty!

Some of her excitement in her daughter's visit evaporated. Without enthusiasm, Katherine showed the young couple the rest of the house, and then their bedrooms. Tony was to sleep in the one which had been used by Pat during his leave. Judy would have the small spare room separated from her mother's by a new modern bathroom.

Judy's quick eye noted the flowers on her dressing-table, and she suddenly turned to her mother and said impulsively:

"Thanks awfully, Mummy. It looks *sweet* and such a treat after London."

"I'm glad you like it, darling," said Katherine.

Then quickly Judy covered up her moment of sentiment by adding:

"What luxury, eh, Tony? Spring mattresses, super bathrooms, soft carpets, and all that food downstairs! You and I'll have to come down here occasionally to see how the rich live. We've got to get used to slumming."

Katherine winced.

"I hope not," she said in a low voice.

"She's pulling your leg, Mrs. Tracy," said Tony with a laugh. "As a matter of fact, the pair of us, if we pool our resources, won't do too badly. The main difficulty is finding a couple of rooms, or even one, not too far from the centre of things, at a reasonable price these days."

"Yes, I know," said Katherine.

Judy avoided her mother's gaze now. They were touching dangerous ground. Hurriedly she said:

"Tony, let's take Pip and Squeak for a walk and see the countryside before the sun goes. I'd like to stroll over and have a look at the Thatched Cottage."

"Yes, do, darling," said Katherine brightly. "Mrs. Clarke,

140

who lives there now, is an awfully nice girl, and they've got a Corgi puppy who adores Pip and Squeak. Introduce yourself and see how the old place is looking."

But after they'd gone, and she watched the two straight, slender figures disappear through the trees, Katherine sat down and smoked a cigarette and did some serious and anxious thinking. Robert was right. Tony couldn't be nicer, and would one day make a successful doctor, she was sure. Judy was very much in love with him and he with her. And she *must* stop thinking of them as "children." They could and would manage on what they had got, even if it meant "slumming," as Judy put it. But she could still feel that Judy's whole life and sense of balance had been disturbed by her mother's second marriage. She still mistrusted the real reason for Judy's desire to rush things, instead of settling down to a quiet sensible term of engagement.

That night, with Robert present, the subject came up. (Of course it *had to* . . . that's what Judy and Tony had come down for.) And it was Robert who tactfully and wisely brought the conversation round to the future while they were drinking their coffee and smoking their after-dinner cigarettes.

He addressed himself to Tony. The Collie, with feminine fickleness, had momentarily transferred her attentions from her master to the young medical student, and sat on her haunches while Tony pulled her ears, slavishly regarding him. Robert said:

"What would be the direct effect upon you, at the hospital, if you suddenly got yourself married?"

Tony looked up quickly. Judy stiffened, and cast a rapid glance at her mother, who changed colour slightly. Tony answered:

"In what way, sir? Do you mean what effect would it have on my work or my financial position?"

"Both," said Robert.

"Financially there would be no change. One doesn't get allowances for marriage as in the Army," said Tony, grinning. "I shall just continue to get my grant, out of which I have to pay my various fees, buy my books, etc., but I've got this fiver a week of my own. As far as the work goes, marriage will help rather than hinder, because I shall no longer be in a state of 'flap' about Judy, and no doubt my nagging wife will quieten me down considerably and I shall cower in a corner with my books and be afraid to budge."

This brought a laugh from the rest of the party, with the exception of Katherine, who felt rather as she looked—solemn. Yet, with her own sense of humour asserting itself, suddenly remembered the last line of the famous recitation about "Sam and his Musket":

" *'Let battle commence.'* "

Robert had fired the opening shot. Now came a volley of repartee from both Judy and Tony, each in turn eagerly announcing how much better it would be from every angle once they were married. They would *manage*, Judy kept on saying. *Fleurette* was doing so well that she, Judy, would soon get a rise. Their united incomes would suffice provided they were careful and practical. They didn't want to spend money. Neither of them had extravagant tastes. Tony was even willing to give up smoking. They could *manage*. . .

Judy spoke in a high, excited voice, her large eyes shining with her intensity. The mother listened and watched and *feared*. All very well to be so much in love, so young and self-confident. But would it be *right* to allow Judy to enter without further thought into this most serious of all contracts? Only nineteen . . . and Tony, the first man in her life . . . and she had had so much lately to influence her towards marrying in haste and repenting at leisure!

Deeply troubled, Katherine looked from her daughter to the young man. Oh, he was so nice and so good-looking, and so amusing. She admitted all that and she was sure he would work hard and pass his exams. But they had no money. She, Katherine, could not do much for Judy; she might be able to scrape up a trousseau, but it would be a modest one. There was still Pat's future to be thought of—when he left the Army there must be a nest-egg waiting for him. He might want a little capital, and under no circumstances would Katherine count on help from Robert. He would offer it, but neither of the children would accept it, even if Katherine could bring herself to do so, she knew that. Besides, they were not Rob's responsibility. David had been their father, and *she* was still their legal guardian.

"I loathe living alone in digs, and it will be such fun to have a little home with Tony!" she heard Judy say in a fervent voice, then added, "And we just mustn't have children at once . . . until we can afford them. . . ."

Kathering put her tongue in her cheek. "*Oh, Judy, Judy, how little you know about life and marriage, and how many girls have said the same thing and started to produce a family within a year!*"

Restlessly, Katherine got up and walked to the other end of the room, making pretence that she had seen a flower out of water that must be put back. She wanted to hide her anxiety. She did not *want* to be a wet blanket . . . to spoil this reunion with Judy which was still so delicate and brittle, so liable to break with one wrong touch. She kept trying to tell herself that the financial question did not really arise. The thing that held *her back* was that motive for this rushed marriage.

Then she heard Judy say:

"As a matter of fact, we've talked things over, Tony and I, and we think it would be silly to have a lot of money wasted on a wedding . . . I mean the sort of 'white bride and champagne' do. All that expense. We'd just like to slip quietly into a little church in town and perhaps have a weekend's honeymoon; and we'd ask for cheques instead of wedding presents. . . . I mean the old salt cellars and spoons which won't be of much use until we can get a proper home of our own. . . ."

Then Katherine swung round, her eyes full of resentment. Must she be robbed even of the thrill of seeing Judy as a "white bride" and of giving her a proper send-off?

"If you get married, surely you'd like it to be from your own home and in Cooltye Church!" she exclaimed.

Judy avoided her gaze and answered:

"I couldn't possibly expect Unc . . . Robert . . . to have a wedding palaver here, and I don't really want one even if he is generous enough to allow it, thanks, Mummy. I admit that Tony and I are going to have a struggle, so we'd far better start off quietly and with no splash. We'd neither of us like a register office. Just a quiet church affair, but with you and . . . and of course Robert . . ." she cleared her throat, "and Pat, and Tony's relations. It would be better away from Cooltye, where everybody knows me, and there would be such a fuss."

Katherine's heart sank to its lowest ebb. So Judy meant to carry her fight right into the very heart of things . . . right into her *mother's heart*. Stab after stab thrust into it—unmeaningly, no doubt; it was just her mulish obstinacy and independence—that *hatred* that Judy had developed, of being organized or cosseted. That infernal pride! She was courageous. She was consistent. Katherine had to admire her even while she found the child exasperating.

Robert said:

"Well, I'm sure I'd be very pleased for you to look on this as your home, and be married from here if you'd like it, Judy."

Judy and Tony together thanked him, but each in turn said that they would prefer an absolutely quiet wedding in town. (Tony backed Judy up in this because he knew that nothing would ever induce her to accept Robert's offer.)

Then Judy turned to her mother, two red spots on her cheeks.

"We haven't got your permission yet, Mummy, so all this talk is a little previous, isn't it?"

"Perhaps," said Katherine.

Tony advanced and, hands in his pockets, gave Judy's mother his most beguiling smile.

"Please trust me with her, Mrs. Tracy."

"I would do that willingly," exclaimed Katherine, "if I wasn't afraid that she is rushing into it because her home life has changed."

There it was, *out*, in the open . . . and the whole room became charged with electricity. Judy immediately broke out:

"Mummy, please don't let's start all that over again. Your marrying again has *nothing* to do with it."

Katherine, trembling a little, looked straight into her daughter's flashing eyes. She said:

"Is that strictly true, Judy?"

Judy opened her lips, shut them again, clenched her hands, then with her innate honesty, said:

"I dare say it isn't *absolutely* true, but no matter what our reasons are, Tony and I want to get married. Please, Mummy, don't try and organize my life any more. It isn't fair!"

Silence for a moment. Tony slid an arm round the girl, quick to give her unspoken support. They stood there, close together, facing Katherine; so young, so defiant, yet so pathetic in their way, thought the mother. She was weary of the whole fight. Yet she found it so hard to give in and so insupportable to imagine that she was the real cause of Judy's rushing precipitously into this thing, and it *might* wreck her whole life.

She made a last appeal.

"Won't you two consider an engagement . . . say for even six months?"

Judy and Tony exchanged glances. Robert Tracy, feeling that he had done his bit and must now keep out of it, leaned forward and knocked his pipe against the fender. He pitied Katherine. He knew that she was suffering. He pitied Judy, too. And he felt uncomfortable because he knew he could not deny all guilt since he had persuaded Katherine to leave her children for him—if *leave them* it could be called.

Then, as the young pair made no answer, Katherine said:

"I see you don't want an engagement."

"We'd much rather not," said Tony in a low voice. "If you could try and understand things from our point of view, Mrs. Tracy."

Katherine swallowed and turned away.

"I'll give you my answer in the morning," she said in a muffled voice.

But she gave it long before that, for after another debate alone with Robert, who, whilst sympathizing with her, still begged her to give Judy her head, she went along to her own room, and passing Judy's door saw a light. Judy was still awake, no doubt worrying her little heart out.

Katherine pushed open the door. Judy had the bedside lamp on and was reading. She put down the book as her mother entered and eyed her with that wariness which was so new to Katherine and so hurtful.

"Oh, Judy!" she broke down. "Do you want this immediate marriage so much?"

"Yes, Mummy, I want it terribly," the girl answered, and then threw the book aside and added with all the pleading in the world, "Do let us get on with it, Mummy, and stop worrying."

Katherine sat on the edge of the bed. She said in a choked voice:

"You'll never make me believe that you wouldn't have had a nice formal, *normal* engagement if we'd been still at the Thatched Cottage."

"Well, darling Mummy, we don't happen to be there, so it doesn't come into it," said Judy, with that awful logic which struck chill at Katherine's sentimental heart.

"And you won't consent to a nice wedding from here?"

Judy was silent a moment. What she would like to have said was:

"I would gladly be married in Cooltye if you were alone . . . if, for instance, Robert was away. But I know that Robert would start acting the magnanimous stepfather, standing in the pew beside you, Mummy; and still worse, expecting me to like it while he did all the duties in Daddy's place; making me walk up the aisle on his arm. No, no not that, whatever else happens!"

But she did not say these things because she had no wish to hurt her mother any more, and she was genuinely grateful because Katherine was trying to be just, and because Robert had extended sympathetic interest.

So she just said, quite sweetly:

"I'm sorry, Mummy let us do things our own way. We don't *want* a proper wedding down here. Just a quiet one where nobody knows us. We might as well begin as we mean to go on—in obscurity until Tony's made his way."

Then Katherine, at last, acknowledged defeat. Turning from Judy, she looked blindly at the parchment shade of the lamp. A moth had got caught inside and was circling frantically round the hot bulb.

"That's how we go on . . . rushing round and round, searching for a way out, and half killing ourselves in the effort," thought Katherine with a sudden sense of complete frustra-

tion. Everything that she had ever planned for this young daughter of hers seemed to have gone awry.

Then she looked up at Judy and said:

"All right, my dear. As you said downstairs . . . it isn't fair of me to withhold my permission. I give in. Have it your own way."

Judy's cheeks burned crimson.

"Then we can count on your permission, Mummy?"

"Yes," said Katherine.

Judy flung her arms round her mother's neck.

"Mummy, you're an *angel*! Honestly, I'm terribly grateful and thrilled."

Katherine hugged her and kissed her back, her eyelids wet with tears. She could not speak. She felt too much bitterness in this moment. For it was a bitter defeat. None of Judy's nor Tony's optimistic schemes for the future, or their assurances, could allay her maternal anxieties.

Judy's kisses and Judy's gratitude comforted her a little. But even now that Judy had got her way Katherine knew that the girl was still not prepared to accept Robert as a stepfather in the true sense of the word, or be married from Cooltye Farm. It was a great blow, and the fight was still on.

13

Six months later.

The shrill remorseless bell of an alarm clock woke Judy out of a profound sleep. She stirred, groaned, reached out a hand and switched off the bell, then, as awakened fully to consciousness, sat up and rubbed her eyes.

Heavens! What a deathly morning, she thought, and how deathly she felt! There was no other word for it. She shivered as the icy morning air struck her warm young limbs and, yawning, reached out for her dressing-gown. When she got out of bed her teeth began to chatter.

"Temperature must be below zero this morning," she muttered.

Then she looked at the bed which she had just so reluctantly vacated, saw a crumpled pillow and a pair of striped blue and white pyjamas. She blinked.

"Gosh, where's my husband?"

The next moment Tony, half dressed and unshaven, came in bearing two mugs of tea, and a look of pious satisfaction on his face.

"Good morning, Mrs. Chapman, madam. I trust you slept well? I am the new butler-cum-handyman."

Judy giggled.

"Honestly, Tony, I don't know how you can be so facetious at this hour of the morning. Its *freezing*, and I feel awful."

Tony set the tea down on the bedside table, which was, in fact, a packing case standing upon its side, to which Judy had nailed a chintz frill. It was a bit rough and ready like the rest of the room, furnished with odd "bits and pieces." It was quite a big pleasant room, with two windows and a cupboard. The paint was new—a fresh green. Judy's own dressing-table and chair and small desk had been sent up from Sussex by Katherine. The gate-legged table and chairs came from Mrs. Chapman. The carpet was old, but still good, and also green—from Mr. Chapman's former office. Two long painted shelves held all their books. The nicest things were the curtains—tomato-coloured chintz with a white design—a wedding present from Elizabeth. Of course there were lots of other presents—one picture, a wrought-iron standard lamp and a couple of easy chairs. Through a small door was a kitchenette and another cupboard. This was their "flatlet" in one of those tall, narrow buildings in a quiet square leading off the Earl's Court Road.

It was certainly not a luxury flat. Even the bathroom had to be shared with the young couple who had a similar "flatlet" upstairs, but it was their *own*, and they could lock themselves in it and feel kings of their small castle. And that means a lot to a young couple who are deliriously in love and have been married for only five months.

Judy hugged her husband, thanked him for the tea, and then, with an arm tucked through his, walked with him to one of the windows. They looked out at incipient gloom. Darkness; sleet driving against the panes, and a bitter wind tossing the bare, soot-blackened boughs of the trees in the square. They were high up—almost at the top of the house. When they had moved in last summer they had been so thrilled because they could see such an expanse of sky. But they had found it very hot. Now they found it very cold!

"Darling, you haven't been feeling at all well lately, have you?" said Tony, his brows knit. "Are you sure——"

"Yes, I'm absolutely sure," Judy cut in quickly, and chewed rather angrily at her lower lip.

Tony cast his eyes heavenwards.

"Angels and ministers of grace . . . defend us!" he gulped.

Judy tried to giggle again but failed; petrified that she might suddenly burst into tears because she felt so stupid and off-colour, she made a bee-line for the kitchen.

"I must get dressed and make your coffee. . . ."

"Hi!" Tony called after her. "Your tea, sweetie."

He carried the mug to her, and after she had filled a saucepan with water and placed it on the gas stove she drank down the tea, warming her cold hands against the mug. Tony rubbed his hair and frowned again.

"You certainly look a bit washed-up, sweetheart."

"Oh, go and shave, and stop worrying about me!" she snapped to cover her own anxiety.

She didn't want *him* to be worried. He was facing one of the most important of his exams at the hospital. He had worked so hard for it, she thought. Sometimes he looked much worse that she did—far too thin and pale—and she felt a sense of guilt because he *didn't* eat quite as well nowadays as he used to do at home in Draycott Avenue. Mrs. Chapman had been right about that. Judy wasn't an awfully good cook. And it wasn't always easy to find time to hunt for sensible and suitable food when one was working oneself all day. It meant tearing out to the shops just before *Fleurette* closed, and everything else closed about the same time.

But as Judy made Tony's coffee and some toast, struggling into her clothes at the same time, her thoughts turned mainly to Cooltye; to her mother.

They were quite good friends these days. She had had no direct cause to feel antagonistic since Katherine gave in about the wedding. Several weekends, she and Tony had enjoyed a very much needed and blessed rest at the Farm. And Mummy came up here about once every ten days and took her out to lunch, and had what they call a "natter." They were closer together, perhaps, because Judy was now the only ewe lamb left to Katherine. Pat—just as they had feared—had been posted abroad soon after Judy's wedding. He was now in Malaya, and although Katherine said little, Judy knew how much she worried about him.

Robert had been behaving awfully nicely—always most hospitable—and hadn't, as Judy feared, offered to "give her away" on the famous wedding day. In fact, Fate had come to all their rescues and landed Robert with a touch of gastric 'flu two days before the wedding, so Katherine attended it alone, and it was she who had given away her daughter. So it had all been as Judy had wanted—extremely quiet, with no fuss, and without Robert.

But of course Katherine's eyes had held a slight touch of reproach during the ceremony, which had got under Judy's skin. She knew that she *ought* to have allowed Mummy to enjoy her daughter's wedding and that she, Judy, had prevented it. Tony's parents had been a bit gloomy about the whole proceedings, too. All of them so set in their ideas and forgetting that they had ever been young themselves, Judy had said to Tony at the time.

Yet here she was this morning, face to face with the realization that one of the familiar prophecies at least was about to be fulfilled.

Judy was going to have a baby.

It was no good beating about the bush. She had to face up to it now, and it wasn't going to be awfully easy. What *would* they do with an infant in a one-room flatlet without even their own bathroom? They themselves had been supremely happy and (when they were not both too tired) enjoyed their complete independence in their small domain. The sweet intimacy of marriage had brought them still closer together in mind as well as in body. Never for an instant had either of them regretted what both their families had called their "rash and importunate behaviour."

Oh yes, it had been such *fun*, Judy thought, and was lifted out of her depression suddenly by the glorious memories of all that "fun" shared with her young, attractive and clever husband. They just rushed home to each other after their day's work . . . chattered and laughed and exchanged all the reminiscences of the day during supper. Went out for walks in the park in the summer evenings. Queued for cheap seats at a cinema or a play. Counted their pennies and, if they thought they could snatch a bit out of the housekeeping, ate at a small restaurant for a treat or bought something they wanted for their little first "home." Once a week they dined with Tony's parents and sometimes Tony brought one of his medical student friends up here for beer and sausages. So far it had been a gay, carefree, charming life, if a somewhat exhausting one!

But now . . .

Judy's courage failed her a little at the prospect of *now*. Not because she didn't *want* a baby. It would be wonderful, and a great fulfilment—to have a son of Tony's . . . or a little daughter. They would be young parents and they would grow up with their child, so all the better able to understand his or her point of view. And, of course, it would be the most beautiful and clever child in the world, and the most healthy. *But* . . . and there was always that *"but,"* pondered Judy as she carried the tray with Tony's and her own breakfasts to the gate-legged table.

They hadn't wanted or meant to have an infant just yet. And she couldn't help squirming at the memory of Mummy shaking her head about the possibility when they first discussed marriage. Even Robert had suggested that a child might make it impossible for her to be a wage-earner according to plan. Difficult for Tony, too, with his eight pounds a week out of which he had to spend so much on his training.

Judy knew, deep down in her heart, that what she really dreaded was not the baby or the struggle . . . but the nodding heads and wagging tongues which would say: *"There you are, what did we say?"* It had the immediate result of making her feel disinclined to go down to Cooltye, which they had planned to do next weekend. She just *couldn't* face Mummy yet. . . . Mummy was no fool. She'd soon see how Judy was looking.

Tony, fully dressed now, smoothing back his hair, walked into the room and grinned at her.

"The future Dr. Chapman at your service, madam. Is your pulse bad? Is your tongue coated? Have you a liver? Can I prescribe some salts? . . ."

"Oh, shut up, darling!" broke in Judy.

Immediately he grew solemn. He fancied he heard a break in his young wife's voice. He knew Judy too well now either to be sympathetic or inquisitive. In her own good time she would be weak and he would comfort her. But he respected her desire to be courageous. And he shared all her fears and doubts about the future.

When she was dressed and seated opposite him, eating nothing, he said gently:

"Try and manage a piece of toast, poppet. You're a working girl, you know, and it's darned cold out. You don't want to work on an empty stummick."

She tried to laugh.

"I'm not hungry."

He pushed the toast towards her.

"Come on . . . have a go!"

She took a slice of toast—began to butter it frugally. He saw her lips trembling. He added:

"You wouldn't like a couple of days with your Mamma, would you?"

Her head shot up.

"Why ever should I?"

"Just if you're not feeling awfully fit, darling, I know Liz would give you a couple of days off and now there's central heating down at Cooltye it's terrifically warm and comfortable there. I thought, perhaps, it might do you good —all the farm butter and milk and eggs."

She looked at him, her eyes soft with love.

"And who would take care of you, might I ask?"

He grinned.

"The blonde from upstairs might come down and feed me."

"Not on your life!" she laughed back. She felt better. It didn't do to start being too serious or give way to weakness, either mental or physical, in these hard times, she reflected grimly. A good laugh is the only way to get through life, and thank goodness Tony had such a sense of humour.

But she explained gently that she had no wish to leave him for forty-eight hours. Not that she hadn't grown rather attached to Cooltye Farm. She had, and Mummy was trying hard, poor darling, not to treat her as if she was still a child.

Tony made no further comment about her *malaise*. He was being tactful, which she appreciated. It was she who flung her arms round his neck just before he left and whispered:

"Don't worry about me, Tony darling. I'll be all right. What is to be *is* to be, and we can take it."

"Gosh, you're a brave girl!" he said admiringly, and looked with utter devotion down into her large bright eyes. Then with a quick kiss he was gone.

Judy made the bed, none too well—she was in such a hurry—threw the gay Algerian spread over it (it made the divan look like a sofa during the day), hastily put the dirty crockery in the wash-up bowl in the sink, then seized hat, coat and bag and ran down three flights of stairs.

Even though she worked for her own sister-in-law she never liked taking advantage of the fact, and was seldom late for her job.

As she boarded a bus for the Brompton Road, wet and cold after waiting in the long, maddening queue, her thoughts continued to turn anxiously towards the future.

This time next year, of course, Tony would have qualified and then he could start to make money, so she hadn't really much to worry about so far as finance went. It was only the next six or eight months which would be a struggle . . . until their child was born and for a while afterwards. For of course she would have to leave *Fleurette* in two or three months' time. That meant saying good-bye to the very valuable five pounds a week which she earned. How silly it all was! With all the will in the world one could make plans, have courage to carry them out, then find the plans all upset by a fresh set of circumstances. Plenty of people had babies and managed in a one-roomed flat. But it wouldn't be very good for Tony with his need for quiet study. And it wouldn't be easy for *her*.

"We'll just have to find something bigger before next spring," Judy thought despairingly. It was inevitable that her mind turned now with some of the old resentment to the thought of her mother's second marriage. For if Mummy had still been living alone in the Thatched Cottage, how thrilled she would have been to have Judy down there for a time . . . and at the prospect of this first grandchild. No doubt, once she recovered from the initial shock of the news, she would be thrilled even now. But always, in the background, lurked Step-papa, thought Judy grimly. She would die rather than foist herself and a child on *him*.

When she reached *Fleurette*, Elizabeth, who was opening the shop, cast a critical look at Judy and said:

"You look like a bedraggled kitten this morning. Don't you feel well?"

"Never better," said Judy, tight-lipped and smiling.

But before she went to lunch after a morning's work she had to confess to a—'not so well' feeling. And then, with Elizabeth's critical gaze upon her, muttered:

"I suppose you'll have to know sooner or later, only for

heaven's *sake* don't tell your parents. Time enough when we've decided what to do."

Elizabeth, alternating between the desire to be sympathetic and feeling apprehensive, went pink in the face and said:

"You two are the *limit*. I thought you weren't going to have a family until Tony qualified."

Judy muttered:

"We thought so, too."

Elizabeth shook her head.

"You *have* been and gorn and done it, you silly little thing."

Defiant to the end, Judy said:

"What if I have? I think it's *wonderful*."

"You have got guts, I must say," said Elizabeth, and suddenly bent and kissed her young sister-in-law, adding, "I think you're rather wonderful, but it's going to be a bit hard on both of you, isn't it?"

"We aren't the first young couple without any money to have a baby quickly, and I expect we'll manage."

"I just can't imagine Tony as a father."

"I can. He'll be *marvellous*. He often says he'd like to specialize in sick children, if he gets the chance," said Judy.

Elizabeth pouted and laughed.

"Fancy turning *me* into Aunty Liz! And *you* only just twenty as a mother! Its fantastic!"

Judy bit her lip.

"Don't, Liz! You sound like Mummy."

"Are you going to tell her?"

Judy, hands in the pockets of her coat, stared through the flowers out of the window, out at the rain which was still falling steadily. The streets looked hatefully bleak and cold.

"Not yet," at length she answered. "We really don't want anybody to know. You're the only one who does, anyhow."

"Its safe as the Bank of England with me, darling," said Elizabeth. "And now let's go and have some food. You look *starved*."

But Judy knew that her "secret" was bound to be out before long. These things can seldom be quiet for long. And Katherine Tracy was a discerning woman.

A month later when she visited London one cold February

morning, she discovered the truth, and it was Judy's own carelessness which was responsible.

She had not really dared to see her mother this month because she felt so seedy and looked so ill. She was afraid of facing Katherine. But Katherine telephoned to the shop to say that she was to be in London next morning with Robert and would call in at Judy's "flatlet" for an hour alone between five and six. She was meeting Robert for dinner later on, in the West End. They were, in fact, celebrating Robert's birthday.

Judy could not say "I don't want to come down," for, in fact, she had never really longed to see her mother more.

It was not until Judy, the scatterbrain, got home that she remembered she had left her knitting out on the table.

When she entered her room she saw her mother (looking very lovely and smart in a new fur coat) sitting by the gas fire *knitting*. Yes, actually carrying on with the tiny white matinée coat which Judy had just started. Judy was not very good at knitting, and Tony had been laughing at her efforts last night: protesting at the smallness of the jacket which was to encase the limbs of his future son or daughter . . . already known as the "Atom."

Judy closed the door behind her. Her face blushed bright scarlet. She took off her beret and scowled at the knitting.

"Hello, Mummy . . . so sorry I wasn't here to greet you. . . ."

Katherine put down the ball of white wool and the bone needles. Her own face was a little pink. She had to confess that the sight of that knitting had startled her, to say the least of it. Her heart had sunk when she realized its implication. It hardly seemed possible . . . Judy . . . *Judy* . . . her little girl . . . with a baby or her own!

Yet she could confess to a thrill of excitement—of pride. She was going to have a grandchild. *She* would be "Granny" —oh, what a lovely thought—what a profoundly moving one, and wonderful to know that she need not, like so many women who married for the second time, be afraid to tell her second husband about this new status. It would not make her any older in Robert's sight—or any less desirable—she knew that.

The next moment her compassionate gaze was taking in the fact that Judy looked grey and exhausted, despite the proud challenge of the tilted chin, and Katherine moved quickly forward and enfolded Judy's slim figure in a hug that was wholly maternal and without repressions.

"Judy . . . *darling* . . . I am so *glad*."

For an instant Judy was taken aback; too amazed and even confused by her mother's unexpected attitude to think straight. Katherine went on huskily:

"It's *too* wonderful for you. It doesn't matter how difficult it may all be. I can just imagine how *thrilled* you are. I know exactly how I felt when I found out that I was going to have Pat!"

Now she released Judy and moved back a pace, still smiling. Judy changed colour rapidly, then gave a nervous little laugh.

"You're taking a lot for granted, Mum darling! I *might* be knitting for a girl-friend, you know."

"But you're not."

"No, I'm not," Judy admitted in a low voice.

Then suddenly, for no reason in the world except that she was desperately tired, and feeling, as she termed it, "het up," she sat down on the edge of the divan and burst into tears.

Afterwards she said to Tony:

"It really was imbecile of me. I might have had something to cry about if Mummy had done the '*I told you so*' act, and moaned about the whole thing, but she was absolutely grand. Honestly delighted, although I know that she was anxious for me. . . ."

Yes, Judy found her mother at her absolute best that bitter winter afternoon. She did not even give way to the luxury of weeping with a Judy in an unusually weak, emotional mood. She just patted her on the back and said:

"That's right, darling, have a good cry and get it off your little chest while I make you a nice cup of tea."

Judy snuffled into her handkerchief, blew her nose and watched helplessly whilst Katherine threw off coat and hat and bustled round. She brought in two mugs of hot strong tea from the kitchenette . . . produced a home-made cake from the Farmhouse . . . found another shilling for the gas meter (for of course it went out right in the middle of boiling the kettle), and then they sat together in front of the fire, and Katherine watched and smiled while Judy ate the cherry cake ravenously and drank three mugs of tea. It was a relief to her to watch the colour steal back into Judy's cheeks. With her roughened curls and shiny nose and those red-rimmed eyes she looked so much like the young Judy who had, in the old days, just indulged in a fight with her brother, then come to Katherine to straighten it out. It was harder than ever for her to believe that this same Judy would soon be having a child of her own.

Judy was now ready to pour out confidences, grateful, full of renewed admiration for her mother. She capitulated far enough to admit that "the next year might be a bit trying." That was putting it mildly, to Katherine's way of thinking, but she let Judy put what emphasis she wanted on the matter.

She was determined to be tactful and sympathetic and she put over none of the "sob stuff" act that Judy had dreaded. She was practical and encouraging.

"You won't feel dealthy much longer, darling, so cheer up. You're a strong and healthy girl, and I expect you'll soon feel better than you've ever felt in your life before. You must just take a bit more care and try to eat regular meals. My word! I wish I had you down at the Farm and could look after you!"

Judy, feeling replete after that enormous tea, and quite happy all of a sudden, lit a cigarette, then put it out at once.

"No, I'm going to give up smoking," she said firmly.

Katherine glanced around the room. It was quite attractive really. Judy had inherited her flair for *décor*. But just *one room*! When Katherine thought of the size of Cooltye Farm . . . and all that wasted space . . . it was disheartening what a lot these young people had to put up with today! And really they were astoundingly plucky and willing to pay the heaviest price for their independence. One could not help admiring them, but she did wish Judy could get rid of her "complexes" about Robert.

"I suppose you wouldn't like to come down and stay at the Farm for a while?" she asked wistfully.

"It's sweet of you, Mummy, but I couldn't possibly leave Tony."

"He couldn't come up to town every day?"

"Not possible. He has to be at the hospital early and often stays very late."

Katherine looked reflectively at her young daughter.

"How *are* you going to manage, Judy?"

"I'm not quite sure," said Judy with a slight laugh.

"Is it at all possible for you to find a bigger flat?"

Judy explained that there was little hope. Cheap flats were at a premium. They had only got this one because it had been occupied by a former medical student at Bart's who had managed to pass it on to them when he left London.

"But, darling, you can't have the baby *here!*"

Now Judy giggled.

"I must admit it'll be a bit of a squash, and awful having to keep a pram three flights downstairs, and simply sickening having no private bathroom. That's the big snag. It was all right when we were just our two selves."

Katherine forbore to make the obvious comment here. But she *did* wish that these two young things had waited a while. And she felt a trifle reluctant to go back and tell Robert that Judy had done the one thing he had prophesied she'd do. (Dear, far-seeing Robert!)

Mother and daughter discussed the situation for a while longer. Judy said that she hadn't really made any plans except that she knew that she could have the baby under the National Health Scheme, which would cost them nothing, and she would get regular attention from a clinic, and Katherine had nothing to worry about. With a quizzical smile Katherine said:

"But of course I shall!"

Then they laughed together. Judy felt more at ease with her mother than she had done for many long months. And when Katherine begged her to go down to the Farm with Tony for the weekend she secretly retracted her decision *not* to go, and accepted the invitation.

Then with a flash of the old Judy, on the defensive, added:

"But don't let Robert lecture Tony or anything ghastly, will you?"

Katherine stood up and reached for her coat.

"My darling Ju . . . can you imagine Robert doing such a thing?"

Judy gave a short laugh.

"He lectured me once. . . ."

"Are you going to hold that against him for ever?" asked Katherine sadly. "It was only because he thought you weren't being nice to me, and you know how much I mean to him . . ." she broke off, colouring faintly . . . "he's so very good to me, Judy darling, and sweet about you and Pat— you ought to be pleased."

"Oh, I am glad he is so nice to you, Mummy darling," said Judy with unaccustomed warmth, and impulsively came forward and kissed her mother. Now that was so like the old Judy that Katherine felt dangerously sentimental, but knowing her Judy hastily turned the conversation back to the thrilling future.

"When do you think it'll be?"

"Oh, I should think the end of July or beginning of August."

Katherine sighed.

"Just imagine! But with a baby, what I'd like you to have is a little cottage in the country."

"So would I!" said Judy, echoing the sigh. "But I don't see Tony and me realizing such an ambition for a long time."

"What do you want—a boy or a girl?"

"A boy," said Judy at once, and added with a giggle, "I don't think much of daughters, do you?"

"I think a daughter is a wonderful thing to have, and I've always adored mine," said Katherine fervently.

Judy softened towards her mother still more.

"Well, if it is a girl, I shall call it Katherine after you, Mummy."

"And if it's a boy . . . bring the name David into it," said Katherine softly.

"You know I will. I'd love it to be called after Daddy, and I'm sure Tony will agree."

To cover another emotional moment, Katherine said with a laugh:

"Won't our Uncle Pat be thrilled when he hears?"

"Uncle Pat!" said Judy derisively. "Can you *believe* it?"

Then Katherine, full of solicitude, dared to impress it upon Judy that if she wanted "a few pounds" at any time, she must let her mother know.

"Robert is very good to me, and I've got my own little bit of money and the royalties on my books. In fact I could easily make you a regular allowance if you'd accept one, darling."

"Oh, I couldn't possibly!" exclaimed Judy, crimson. "Thanks all the same, Mummy, but Tony and I don't want to take money from anybody, honestly. You do understand, don't you?"

Katherine did understand. But with feminine guile she reflected upon the number of lovely things she could buy in a baby shop, for instance, and have sent to Judy. She was privileged to send presents as the "Granny." There would be a lot of time in the winter evenings down at the Farm, too, for knitting.

Mother and daughter parted on terms of renewed cordiality.

Of course Judy told Tony all about it when he got home much later that evening. By that time she was in bed. It was one of Tony's late nights. When she saw how nipped with the cold he looked, and how tired, she insisted upon getting out of bed and making him some hot coffee. He sat on the edge of the bed and drank it gratefully.

"What a wife!" he exclaimed.

Judy wrinkled her *retroussé* nose. She was huddled in a blue woolly jacket. She had washed and set her hair this evening, and it was tied up in a scarf. Her face was greasy.

"Portrait of glamour girl!" she giggled.

"You're my glamour girl," said Tony. Then, sniffling proudly, "*And* the mother of my first child."

Judy goggled at him.

"First? How many am I going to have?"

"Between ten and twelve," said Tony.

"You may leave me," said Judy coldly, "never to return. I have gruesome visions of myself pushing twins in a pram followed by streams of little toddlers all yelling while I queue for the kippers!"

This picture brought a yell of laughter from Tony. He choked, set down his cup on the table, then put one of her hands against his cheek.

"I *do* love you, Judy."

She kissed the hand blissfully.

"I love *you!*"

"Still happy on nothing a week? Struggling with an infant in a joint like this?" he asked a trifle dismally.

"I'd go through anything to be with you. I told Mummy so."

Tony chewed his lip.

"I don't know that I feel too great about this. Perhaps we *ought* to have waited till I could give you and the Atom a proper home."

This brought a stream of protests from Judy, and ended in both of them agreeing that it was altogether a wonderful idea, and that they were going to be proud and contented whatever the odds against them.

Tony said:

"Your mother seems to have been a perfect angel about it."

"She was. She rather amazed me," admitted Judy.

He stroked her cheek with one finger.

"I always told you you were a little hothead and that she was a poppet."

Judy flushed.

"You know I love Mummy, but it was only her refusal to let us marry that put my back up. *And* her marrying Robert Tracy."

"Well, if I were you I should pipe down on that, my sweetie. Robert is a decent chap and has been for, and not against, us all the way along."

Judy's face now was both crimson and mortified. It was a very gentle rebuke, but the first she had ever had from her young husband.

"Oh, Tony, has it all been *my* fault?"

"No, darling. I know you've been upset—but I think it's time to bury the hatchet, and be pleased that your Mamma is so happy."

"I am. I told her so today."

"Though I say it myself, she and Step-papa have been more decent about it than my own people," Tony added with a frown, "except Liz, who is a good wench and loyal to me."

"Well, I dare say it *was* a bit of a blow for your mother, who wanted you to make a brilliant marriage," said Judy, "and to wait until you were Dr. Chapman!"

Tony stood up and began to take off his coat, yawning. He was a little amused by his young wife's remark. He was not by nature cynical—he was far too young and, as yet, too full of illusions. But he was in his way a student of human nature as well as of the human body, and it struck him as being a trifle ironic that Judy should find excuses for her "in-laws" yet have had none in the past for her own mother and step-father. Queer, he reflected, but you were apt to be intolerant with those of your kith and kin with whom you were too close, and could take the broader, kinder vision of an entire stranger.

But he was pleased when Judy told him that she was willing to go down to Cooltye for the weekend. Not so much because he loved the rest and change down there, but because he wanted Judy to get right back on the old footing with her mother, whom he still thought one of the most charming women in the world.

But it was the old, combative, independent Judy who made haste to add that she would *not* accept financial help from Cooltye, no matter in what spirit it was offered.

"I know you agree, darling. We took on these responsibilities off our own bat and we must face them ourselves. I'm quite willing to be friendly with Robert, but it would *kill* me if he started trying to 'make things easier for us'."

He laughed.

"You are a funny little thing!"

"Don't you agree?" she asked anxiously.

"In this case, absolutely," he said with a sincerity which relieved her mind."

She wanted it always to be this way . . . always to be in entire agreement with the young man she had chosen to marry against all advice.

14

At half past twelve on that following Saturday morning Robert Tracy walked into the kitchen to find his Katherine at her favourite occupation—cake-making. He looked fondly at her. He rather liked her with a smear of flour on one cheek, her ash-blonde hair a little untidy, and that pink flush which made her look such a girl. Grandmother, indeed! Judy could produce her child (and of course he had known this would happen!) but she wouldn't be able to turn his Kath into an elderly dame knitting in her corner. Grandmothers didn't seem to be like that these days, anyhow. They were an amazingly young-looking lot, and Katherine was one of the most youthful of them all.

"Oh, you do look cold, Rob!" she greeted him.

He rubbed his red numbed hands in front of the range and stamped his feet. Snow had fallen last night. It certainly was very cold outside, a beautiful white world—but hard on the animals, and he had been having rather an anxious week. Armstrong was down with a chill and Robert had been working till all hours, and up with the lark. At this time of the year it wasn't all honey being a farmer. There had been sickness among some of the cows, and a couple of nights ago they had lost a dozen prize Leghorns after a visit from a fox which was haunting the place and which so far they hadn't been able to trap. There were always these setbacks, including the frustrations of dealing with governmental departments, at the moment. But Robert never grumbled. One of the things that Katherine most admired in him was his philosophic acceptance of misfortune. He said:

"Getting ready for your little lamb and her spouse?"

"That's right," smiled Katherine.

He came up and dropped a kiss on her cheek.

"Granny!"

"Step-grandpapa!" she jeered back.

Robert rubbed his ear.

"You know, Kath, I shall be quite interested in the little blighter. After all, it'll be your flesh and blood, and we could do with another Katherine in the world."

She gave a happy sigh, and her large eyes shone at him.

"You say such lovely things to me, Rob, and I know you mean them, which is even better."

"Of course I mean them."

"Judy was so afraid you might lecture her or Tony."

"Wot, *me?*" Robert asked, grimacing.

"Yes, you," Katherine laughed, and went back to her baking. "Lunch won't be a minute, darling. You've got Lancashire hot-pot. I'm saving the chicken for the children tonight."

"I shan't say a word out of place when they come," he assured her. "But I would like *you* to let those two know that if things get tight when Judy loses her job . . . I'd really like to be of help—as any father might do."

Her heart thrilled to those words, but she shook her head at him.

"Typical of you, Rob, but don't suggest it. Judy's still very touchy, and I do want things to be all right between the three of us now."

Robert sat down and began to pull off his boots.

Then the telephone bell rang.

Katherine had just plunger her hands once more into a basin of cake mixture. Robert hastily rose and, walking in his stockinged feet into the hall, answered the call.

When he came back she was about to ask him what was showing on the television tonight (the set was his latest gift to her), when she stopped. She saw that his whole expression had changed. For Robert, he looked unusually disturbed.

"Who was that?" she asked.

Then her heart seemed to turn over as he walked up to her and took both her hands. She knew at once that something serious had happened.

"Rob! What is it? *Judy* isn't ill, is she . . .?"

He told her without beating about the bush. He knew that Katherine had the courage to face up to anything. It *was* Judy, but it had been Tony who had telephoned, for Judy was in hospital. She had had an accident. Running down the stairs this morning from her flat, she had cought her toe in a piece of worn carpet and stumbled and lost her balance. It was not a serious fall, not even enough to break any bones or sprain an ankle. She had just wrenched her left arm. But the shock and the way in which she had fallen had necessitated her being taken to hospital immediately. The girl in the upstairs flat had heard her calling for help, found her, and telephoned through Tony, who, mercifully, had been able to come at once with the ambulance.

Katherine went quite white as she listened. Her knees shook under her.

"Oh, Rob!" she gasped.

He tightened his hold of her hands.

"It's all right, darling. You know Tony is pretty nearly qualified, and he assured me there is no cause for anxiety, so we can believe him. Poor little Judy has had a bit of pain and misery and so forth, but she isn't in any danger. It merely means, unfortunately, that she has lost her baby."

Katherine's face screwed up as though she were going to cry, but quickly she recovered herself. She drew a deep breath and pulled her hands away from Robert's strong fingers.

"I must go up to town at once."

Robert glanced at his wrist-watch.

"There's the 2.9 from Hassocks—gets you up to Victoria at 3.22. You'll just have time for a bite of lunch."

"I couldn't——" began Katherine.

Robert's deep-set eyes smiled at her. He interrupted:

"Kath, dearest, be sensible. I repeat—young Judy isn't in any danger, and there's no need to panic. Tony was quite definite about that. It's a very cold day and you need some food before you set out on a visit to a hospital. *Please!*"

She was about to protest, then gave in with a short laugh.

"I suppose you're right. But I feel I ought to dash off at once."

"Of course you do. But I dare say if you could see Judy

now she's sleeping quite peacefully, and will be until you get up there."

"She *did* ask for me?" asked Katherine, with such a hopeful look in her eyes that Robert had not the heart to tell her the truth. Judy *hadn't* asked for her. Independent, game to the end, he had thought; Tony had said:

"I'm telling you this off my own bat, sir. As a matter of fact Judy wasn't very keen on her mother knowing, in case she flapped."

Then when Robert had observed somewhat dryly that Katherine didn't "flap" in moments of crisis, Tony had added in a rather sheepish voice:

"I know that. I think the real truth is that Ju is so afraid of a fuss—you know what she's like. And, poor little scrap, she rather feels it's her own fault because she was running down those ruddy stairs."

Robert remembered these words, but did not repeat them to his Katherine. He just said:

"I should think this is the one time a girl would like to see her mother. Anyhow, your place is with her, and Tony was the first to say so."

"Tony's a poppet," said Katherine, and added in a strangled voice, "Poor darlings, what a blow for them!"

"Well, take it easy, my sweet. It may all be for the best, you know."

"Looking at things practically—yes," admitted Katherine.

But her mind went to that basket with the white wool and the pathetic knitting up there in Judy's flat, and it seemed to her the saddest thing in the world that this should have happened. It was too soon for her to feel relieved because Judy would not now have to face all the anxiety and strain of child-bearing without a proper home or adequate means.

She was still sadder about it all when finally she sat beside Judy's bed in the big hospital to which she had been taken by Tony, who met her train. Tony looked ghastly, she thought —worse, poor boy, than Judy herself, although Katherine's heart was stabbed with pain when she first saw her young daughter's face. Judy looked so much *older* lying there on that rigid white hospital bed. Her hair out of curl, clinging damply to her forehead, her lips tightly compressed, her eyes drowsy with the drugs which had alleviated some of her suffering.

Katherine also had to remind herself that she must move with the times and not be shocked to find Judy in a public women's ward. These were the days of National Service. Judy was the wife of a medical student, and Tony could not afford a private room. But she knew better now than to offer to pay for Judy to be moved—even if a private room were available, which was doubtful.

She forced herself to speak with unconcern, as she took off her gloves and put a hand over Judy's.

"Well, you silly old thing. How many times has your mother told you not to run down the stairs. So like you! You always used to dash down the stairs at home two at a time. I used to tell you that one day you'd break your little neck."

Judy gave a twisted smile. She gazed at her mother, who was always a delight to look at. She brought warmth and colour and glamour into the ward. Judy said:

"Oh, Mum . . . isn't it a *rotten* thing to have happened! My poor Atom!"

"Rotten!" agreed Katherine. "And I'm terribly sorry, darling. You know that."

"Yes, I really believe you wanted it," whispered Judy.

"Of course I did . . ." Katherine had to keep a tight hold on herself not to let the tears come into her eyes now, "but——"

"Oh, I know all the things you're going to say. Tony's said them already," broke in Judy, and her own tears began to flow freely through sheer weakness. She had been bitterly disappointed when she had learned the consequences of her fall. "I'm still so *young*, and there's plenty of *time*, and all the rest of it. But think how awful it will be if I *never* have another one."

Katherine laughed.

"Darling, of *course* you will. Lots of them, I expect. I insist on being the grandmother of a huge family—yours and Pat's."

Judy gave one of her giggles, which cheered Katherine

up considerably. She took a handkerchief out of her bag, and gently dabbed the tears on Judy's cheeks. Judy sniffed and said:

"Um! It smells nice, Mummy. You always do. What is it?"

"Some of that heavenly *'Moment Supreme'* which Robert bought me in Paris."

"It's super," said Judy, and held the wisp of cambric against her nose, then added, "How's Robert?"

Katherine thrilled. Never before had Judy condescended to ask in so friendly a fashion after her stepfather.

"He's very well indeed, but terribly hard-worked because Armstrong is laid up and this weather is frightful for farmers."

"But it must look rather nice down at Cooltye with the snow on the ground, and the Downs all white," whispered Judy, with a wistful look in her eyes.

"It is, and you must come down to us as soon as you are able to leave hospital, and let me nurse you up, won't you?"

"It would be nice, but I shan't want to leave Tony."

Katherine accepted this meekly and said:

"Well, darling, don't let's worry about it now. Maybe Tony could get a few days' holiday to come with you and look after his wife."

"We couldn't afford it," said the old Judy.

Now Katherine protested.

"Oh, darling, don't be a little idiot. Give me the pleasure of financing a short holiday for you under my own roof."

It was on the tip of Judy's tongue to say, *"But it's not yours—it's Robert's roof,"* but she curbed it. She had made up her mind to take Tony's advice and stop being hostile towards Robert. She said:

"Who asked you to come up, Mummy?"

Katherine stared.

"Didn't you?"

Then the blunt, outspoken Judy made a diplomatic move for the first time in her young life . . . mainly because she wanted to show Katherine some gratitude for coming all this way up to town to see her on a cold, dreary Saturday afternoon. She smiled and whispered:

"Of course I did. I was dying to see you. You really are too good to me, darling Mummy."

Katherine's eyes shone like stars. As she said to Robert later that evening:

"It really was wonderful to hear Judy speak like that. I saw through it . . . I *realized* that was not Judy but Tony who had sent for me, but Judy didn't want to hurt my feelings. She *has* changed . . . she's absolutely sweet these days, and I think we shall all understand each other better in future. She even asked how *you* were, Rob. I must write and tell Pat. When he went abroad he was rather disturbed about the rift between Judy and myself."

Robert smiled and said:

"I know it would come right. She is a good child at heart, and a brave one. You didn't do wrong to let those two marry, Kath. Personally I think they'll get on top of all their troubles. As for you and Judy—it's only a question of time and adjustment on both sides—yours and hers."

They were sitting in front of a roaring log fire. Robert had made it up all ready for Katherine, knowing that she would be tired and frozen when she got back from London. Mrs. Askell had come in to cook a meal so that she had no work to do tonight, for Katherine was still doing the cooking. They had a Danish maid arriving at the Farm on the first of March, and after that Katherine meant to go back to her typewriter and do another children's book.

Katherine smoked her after-dinner cigarette and looked thoughtfully into the flames. It was good to be back with her husband, and in her home. Cooltye Farm had become very dear to her. Outside, snow was falling again, and a north wind was howling. But the forecast on the radio was good. Tomorrow it might be a calm white world, with sunshine; glittering powdered trees; fresh crystalline air. Sussex at its wintry best.

Her thoughts turned to the daughter who lay up in that hospital ward. Poor little disappointed, struggling Judy. Thank goodness she was so much in love with her young husband, and that he was so much in love and thoughtful for her.

"Oh, Rob, I do want Judy to come down here and convalesce!" at length she exclaimed. "I do *hope* she won't refuse out of sheer pride, and go back to climbing those stairs and being on her feet at the shop too soon."

"Well, don't press it, sweet," said Robert. "Just go at it quietly and casually, and enlist Tony's support, and I dare say you'll get her down here in the end."

Katherine smiled and leaned forward, and laid her hand on his knee.

"You're full of wisdom and understanding, aren't you, my Rob?"

"And you're full of heart and one of the most beautiful women in the world," he replied.

She looked at his lean, strong features, that face, a little gaunt and weatherbeaten, but full of tenderness, and grown inexpressively dear to her.

"You're a very beloved person, Rob," she said.

He put down his pipe, seated himself beside her on the sofa, put his arm round her and then sat with her like that in silence for a long while, dreaming as they watched the fire.

15

JUDY was in one of her "moods."

She was due to leave the hospital in forty-eight hours. She had to face up to the fact that she felt very weak and wobbly now that she was up, and that she really did not relish climbing those three steep flights of stairs up to her flat. The thought of Tony troubled her, too. He was facing his final examinations in ten days' time. He had had a streaming cold for the last two days and had not been quite as cheerful or philosophic as usual. In fact, they had actually snapped at each other when they discussed the future when he visited her last night. It had been a very small "snap" and, like so many lovers' tiffs and matrimonial differences, had arisen out of nothing in particular.

Tony had said that she ought to go down to the Farm, where her mother could look after her. Now Judy, in many ways, wanted to go home (if she was to allow that name to be conferred upon Cooltye Farm). It hadn't been a lot of fun in the ward, where, for the first time in her young life, she had learned the grim meaning of pain and sickness. Where, in spite of all the courage and cheerfulness among women so much worse than herself, there lurked the inevitable shadow of death. She was longing to get away from it. And she wanted to be with Tony. She had missed him terribly. She could not *bear* the thought of leaving the hospital and not going to *him*. She did not want him to encourage a convalescence at Cooltye, so she had said something silly about his "wanting to get rid of her." Tony had blown his nose loudly and said:

"Don't be fatuous!"

She, between set teeth, answered:

"Okay, don't bully me...."

And so on for about five minutes, glaring at each other and talking a lot of nonsense until suddenly they burst out laughing. But Judy, weak and feeling rather stupid, had ended in tears. So Tony, with his arm round her, also ended by saying:

"Poor sweet! She shan't be bullied any more. It's all been beastly for you, and it was all my fault. You shan't be sent to Cooltye if you don't want to go. I'll carry you up the stairs to our flat and you can stay in bed all day and I can look after you when I come home at night."

She had jumped at that. After swearing passionate devotion to each other, they had parted as deeply in love as ever. But after he left her Judy lay awake listening to the noises in the ward, restless, and a little uncertain as to whether she was behaving with wisdom. Oughtn't she to let Mummy come up and drive her down to the Farm (which she so much wanted to do)? Every day a little note from Katherine had come to cheer Judy; the sort of notes that she had adored when she was young, illustrated by small comic sketches, at which Katherine was very clever. The last one had depicted Pip and Squeak in a skirmish with Sally and the farmhouse cat. It was all paws and tails, and made Judy giggle until the woman in the next bed had asked what the joke was about. Then Judy had shown her the little drawing and she had giggled too.

But Judy had steadfastly refused all Mummy's invitations. In her last letter she said:

"Please don't think that it is anything to do with the old feud, Mum. I'd love to come, but I just can't leave Tony all alone. But please thank Robert for asking me and tell him how thrilled I was with that marvellous box of eggs and the two ducks' eggs, which I particularly adore. It was good of him to remember...."

That had brought rather a disappointed letter from Katherine, who seemed obviously very concerned about her. Then, this morning, Tony's mother had paid a visit to her. Judy, privately, hadn't much use for her mother-in-law. She had really very little to talk about except her bridge and her clothes. And although she was extremely pleasant and brought Judy a wonderful bunch of flowers from *Fleurette*, it seemed to Judy that there was always a slight sting behind Mrs. Chapman's geniality.

"I do wish darling Tony wasn't looking so ill," she had remarked. "This was most unfortunate, happening just before his big exam. . . ."

"I'm sure I didn't want it to happen," Judy had answered in rather a surly voice. Whereupon Mrs. Chapman said:

"Oh, I think it's been a *mercy*, really! What *would* you have done with a family in your position?"

Hardly the type of remark to endear her to Judy, although it had been followed by the lightest of laughs from Mrs. Chapman. Then she had said:

"How pretty you look, dear! Your skin's *perfect*. No wonder my boy lost his head over you."

Judy writhed at the memory of that honeyed barb. But as she thought about it on this cold, foggy February morning, when it was so dark in the ward that they had to have the lights on, she felt all the more determined to show Mrs. Chapman and everybody else that she and Tony may both have "lost their heads" temporarily, but they had found them again, and could manage without help from anybody.

She was all the more determined not to go down to Cooltye, which would be an admission, she decided, of weakness . . . an admission that she and Tony needed support.

This afternoon visitors were allowed. She didn't expect any. Tony dropped in at any old time that he was able—he was a great favourite of the Sister-in-Charge of the ward, which was lucky for Judy. Her mother was coming up tomorrow. Even if Judy wouldn't go down to the Farm, Katherine insisted on coming up in the car to take her back to Earl's Court.

Then suddenly, as the ward filled up with visitors, Judy saw a familiar figure—a tall man walking rather gingerly and looking rather awkward—preceded by one of the nurses. Judy stared at him round-eyed. It was Robert Tracy himself.

Judy had just dressed and was sitting on the edge of her bed, furious because she felt so feeble and wretched. She was halfway through a letter to Pat, who seemed to be feeling the heat of Kuala Lumpur and had terrified them all by being in a train which had been held up by bandits, although fortunately he had come to no harm.

"How lovely it will be when you are out of the Army and we can all be together again . . ." (she had just written). *"I miss you, you old so-and-so. Wasn't it a shame about the Atom? Can't think why I had to go and fall down those stairs. Always was a bit weak in the ankles, and am now feeling a bit weak in the head, too. By the way, I'm not so anti-Robert these days. He is really very decent about things, and sometimes I feel a bit guilty. . . ."*

It was at this moment that Judy lifted her head and saw Robert walking towards her. He had a parcel in one hand and a somewhat sheepish smile on his lean, bronzed face. He looked nipped with the cold.

"What a detestable day!" he greeted her. "And we were half an hour late because of the fog. It was thick once we got to Three Bridges. How's the girl?"

Judy knew suddenly that she was glad to see him. One could feel jolly lonely and miserable in a hospital ward, and she had rather envied the others who had visitors. Robert, for the first time that he could remember, saw a light of real welcome in Judy's big blue eyes.

"I say, how terrific to see you!" she exclaimed. "What *are* you doing up in town?"

He sat down on the chair beside the bed and pushed the parcel into her hand.

"My sweet ration for a month. Don't say I'm not a martyr!"

Judy looked down at the box.

"Oh, you shouldn't have! I can't take it. . . ."

"Silly," he laughed. "I don't eat sweets. I smoke pipes, and your mother says she is getting plump, so I'm not going to give them to her."

"I shall start on it right away. You know my passion for sweets," said Judy, and giggled a bit as she untied the string and opened the parcel. . . . "Chocolate peppermint creams! Um! My favourites!"

He took off his coat. He felt suddenly rewarded for having taken this journey. Not that he did not feel a trifle guilty because he had not told Katherine that he was coming to see her daughter. He had invented some story about another Farmers' Conference which was quite fictitious. But Armstrong was back and things were working fairly smoothly on the Farm, so he had felt able to get away. And he had been rather cunning about it . . . no fear that Katherine would offer to come with him, because she had her Women's Institute meeting today, and that was a thing which Katherine never missed. She was very keen on village life. He, on his part, had felt it essential to see and talk to Judy.

He looked around the ward and grimaced.

"Suppose I daren't smoke my pipe!"

"No, you'd better not," she laughed, with a mouthful of chocolate. It was surprising how much more cheerful she felt. Old Robert was really awfully nice. She asked after her mother and the animals, and then added:

"What brought you up?"

Then Robert averted his gaze.

"Well, as a matter of fact, I came up solely for the purpose of talking to you, young lady. Your mother knows nothing about it."

"Talking to me?" repeated Judy, wide-eyed.

"Yes."

"Oh, goodness!" cried Judy childlishly, and felt her cheeks crimson.

He ran a critical gaze over her. He felt full of sudden pity. He had never seen her look more in need of rest and fresh air and good food. Naturally, what she had just been through was enough to make her look ill, but she really did seem a wreck this morning. He said:

"Look, Judy, I'm not going to beat about the bush. I just want to put a few facts before you. Your mother has repeatedly asked you to go down to Cooltye when you leave this place so that she can nurse you up. You've refused . . . mainly, I take it, because you can't yet bring yourself to feel that it's like your old home. But——"

"No, it isn't really that!" Judy interrupted, her breath quickening. "Honestly . . . even if Mummy had still been at the Thatched Cottage I wouldn't have wanted to leave Tony. After all, we haven't been married very long and we don't like being separated."

"I appreciate that, but I wonder, my dear, if you ever stop to look at anything from the other fellow's point of view . . . if I may be brutal for a moment . . . I wonder if you are not inclined to be a bit egotistical?"

To his surprise she accepted the rebuke gamely.

"I think I *am* an egoist," she confessed. "But is it wrong to want to be with the person you love?"

"If it isn't for the good of that person, yes."

"I don't know what you mean."

"Well, look here, I didn't come up to deliver a lecture. . . ."

"Go on, say what you want. . . . I can take it and I dare say I deserve it."

He eyed her with raised brows. This was a new and humble Judy. Her experience of suffering had blunted some of the sharp edges, he thought, and given her more understanding . . . more of that tolerance which the passage of time brings to us all.

"Well, it's like this, Judy," he said. "As I see things, *you* have refused to come down to the Farm both because of your wish to be with your husband and out of your reluctance to accept any kind of help from me. But what about Tony's point of view—and your mother's? Take hers, first. I live with her, you know, so I know how she feels. Ever since you got married she has been deeply anxious for your welfare, but I think you will agree she has tried not to show it or to interfere."

"I admit that," said Judy in a low voice.

"And," Robert went on, "I have kept completely out of it."

"Yes." She nodded.

"But since your accident, your mother has not altogether been able to control her maternal feelings. She has been sleeping badly, and is what I would call "off colour." She talks incessantly of you, and although I know I am giving away secrets, she was actually in tears the other day when she got your last letter saying that you wouldn't convalesce with us. I think she had so looked forward to nursing you up a bit. Don't you think, Judy, that you've punished her enough for marrying again?"

The bluntness of that question seemed to startle Judy. The pupils of her eyes dilated and for a moment she seemed unable to speak, struggling within herself. Then she exclaimed:

"Oh, but I never meant this to be a punishment for Mummy. Honestly! That's unjust. I adore Mummy and she's been simply marvellous to me. I hate to think she was reduced to tears because of anything I wrote."

"Well she was, you know," said Robert gently.

"Oh dear!" whispered Judy, and looked near to tears herself.

"Don't you think that you could bring yourself to let her drive you down to us tomorrow instead of back to your flat, and give her the great happiness of nursing you back to complete health?"

"But there's Tony——"

"Now we're coming to the second part of my argument," broke in Robert with a smile. "The egotism extends a little bit in his direction, doesn't it, Judy, my dear?"

"I don't understand. . . ."

"Well, I saw your young man just now. He happened to be passing through the hall when I came into the hospital. We exchanged a few words. He's got a fiendish cold, by the way. . . ."

"Oh, I know! Poor darling!"

"Well, do you think he's going to be better for having you back at home at the cost of rushing away from his work, perhaps a bit sooner than he ought to do . . . getting overtired . . . and waiting on you . . . because you're obviously not fit to do the shopping or cook the meals . . . whereas if you were with us he would be relieved of all anxiety—go home to his own people and be looked after for a week or so, with no outside distractions to interfere with his work. I think your mother was telling me he takes his Finals in March. The boy needs to be in calm waters at the moment. Naturally he wants to be with you—you're both very much in love. But it's only a question of a couple of weeks out of the whole of your lives. And he could come down to the Farm for the weekend. Do you see what I'm driving at, Judy? If you come to us instead of going back to that flat tomorrow you will be doing a service both to your mother *and* your husband, as well as to yourself."

Silence . . . after what was probably one of the longest speeches Robert Tracy had ever made, for he was not a voluble man. And, having made it, he half regretted it. What *would* his Katherine say to him for coming up here and talking like this to the poor kid when she was not well enough to cope? If she had burst into tears right now and run a temperature he would have only himself to blame.

But Judy did not burst into tears. She sat very quietly for a moment, her hands folded in her lap, her gaze looking past her stepfather, blindly down the ward. She was thinking over every word that he had just spoken. It had all sunk deeply into her consciousness. And curiously enough she did not resent what he had said . . . did not feel at all antagonistic towards him this afternoon, nor resentful because of this sudden and unexpected attack upon her sentiments.

She knew that he was right. He was right and she was wrong. She *had* considered this matter only from her own point of view. Tony wanted her back in the flat with him, but it *would* mean extra work and worry for him when he most needed to be free of it. It *would* be tiring for him, and she *couldn't* look after him. She needed looking after. Yes, Robert was right. Tony ought to go and live at Draycott Avenue, where he would get a warm reception and plenty of spoiling, and she ought to go down to Cooltye to Mummy.

She drew a deep breath.

Robert looked at her and pulled the lobe of his ear. His lean face went a trifle red.

"Have I been and gorn and done it? Do you want to kick me out?" he asked with a whimsical smile.

Then Judy, with the utmost generosity, held out her hand.

"No, on the contrary, Robert, I think you're grand—and I've been a little beast to you. I really do think it is terrific of you to have bothered to come up here and take all the trouble to say these things to me. Especially after I've been so unfriendly."

His heart leaped with gladness, and as he took the thin young hand in his he thought:

"Thank God! You'd never have forgiven me, would you, Kath, if I'd made an enemy of her for life?"

Judy went on:

"You're dead right. Somehow it's taken a bit of straight talking to make me see sense. I *was* being a complete egoist. And I know it's only two weeks out of a lifetime. I'll come down to Cooltye and let Tony go to his old home. After all, it won't be very long till the weekend, then he can join me. But I don't really see why Mummy should want to nurse her horrid, selfish daughter."

Robert laughed.

"She happens to be very devoted to her horrid, selfish daughter."

Judy sighed.

"I feel rather relieved. Much as I adore Tony, it *was* going to be a bit of a bind, getting up all those stairs, and I don't relish the idea of living on sardines at the moment. It'll be absolute heaven being spoiled by Mummy. And, although I can't abide Mrs. Chapman, I know she'll spoil Tony."

"It looks to me as though there'll be a bit of spoiling all round," said Robert.

Judy sighed again.

"Tony will be pleased."

"I rather think he will. He murmured something to me about wishing you would let your mother nurse you up."

"He's terribly sweet to me."

"He's a very nice chap."

"And he *will* do well, and we *shall* be all right a bit later on."

"Of course you will," said Robert.

Another pause. They were both of them feeling a trifle shy of each other. Then Robert said:

"Look here. If you'd like to be alone with your mother for a few days, I dare say I could take a trip up to Aberdeenshire to see an old uncle of mine who's got a lot of sheep up there and might be interested to renew acquaintanceship with me."

Then Judy broke in:

"Robert, don't be as nice as all that . . . honestly! I couldn't bear it. I wouldn't *dream* of letting you leave your own home, and I'm sure you've plenty to do on the Farm. Besides which I don't want you to go. Mummy would be *miserable* without you, and I thought we were trying to make *her* happy."

That answer gave Robert the utmost satisfaction. He stood up and buttoned his coat.

"Then I shall stay there," he said, and grinned at her. "And tick you off if you don't behave yourself and eat everything that's put in front of you. We've got our new Danish maid arriving on Monday. That'll give your mother more time for you."

Judy also stood up.

"I shall look forward to it. Will you ask Mummy to fetch me in the car tomorrow?"

"I couldn't go home with better news," he said.

"And I," said Judy, "think you're a perfect poppet to be so sweet . . . to all of us. . . ."

"Oh, rot!" said Robert, and coughed twice. Then added:

"Do you think it would matter if you don't tell Katherine I persuaded you to come down to us? Tell her I visited you —but no more. Let her think you changed your mind voluntarily."

She realized that he did not want the glory of his small achievement, and liked him all the more for it.

And suddenly, to his intense surprise and embarrassment, she reached up and kissed him on the cheek and said:

"Okay!"

When he told Katherine about the kiss, he said:

"It was the first time in Judy's life that she's ever kissed me, and I am sure that the hatchet is buried between us for good. You know, I felt positively *paternal*. She was as much my daughter as yours in that moment, Kath. And it must have cost her something to climb down from her high horse so completely, poor little thing!"

Could he have seen and heard what happened after he left the ward he might have felt an added thrill of pride. For the woman in the next bed said to Judy:

"That your father? What a fine tall chap, and such a *nice* face."

Whereupon Judy, with heightened colour, replied:

"He is my stepfather, actually. He *is* awfully nice."

"Some 'steps' are and some 'steps' aren't," said the woman significantly, to which Judy answered:

"Well, mine *is* . . . he couldn't be nicer!"

16

ONE bright March morning about a fortnight later Katherine Tracy sat on the edge of Judy's bed and watched her daughter setting her hair. With the utmost admiration she beheld this momentous task . . . a comb being dipped in water . . . little flat curls being made and pinned by Judy's deft fingers, then a scarf tied round her head. Smiling, at length Judy turned from the mirror to face her mother.

"Now I shall put on a coat and go down to the village and do your shopping, Mum. You said you had a chapter to finish, didn't you?"

Katherine nodded. She felt enormously pleased with life this morning. Judy looked so well, and she had made a complete recovery down here, and her face had filled out and regained some of its old rosy colour. She looked, to her mother's eyes, just a schoolgirl again, instead of the young married woman who had recently been through a nasty illness. And Katherine was pleased, too, because of all the lovely things that had lately taken place.

She thought that she would never forget the pure pleasure she had felt when Judy rang her up to say that she had changed her mind and wanted to come down to Cooltye to convalesce, or when she had driven up to fetch the girl and brought her back to the warmth and comfort of the Farmhouse. Tears had glittered on Judy's lashes when she kissed her young husband good-bye (it might have been for years instead of days!), but Tony had looked thoroughly pleased about it all.

"A couple of weeks at the Farm for you is just what the doctor ordered," he had grinned, "and Mamma is killing the fatted calf for me in ye olde homestead, so everything's fine, and I'll see you on Saturday afternoon, darling."

When he came they all had a lovely weekend. Bill and Joyce dropped in for coffee on the Sunday evening, and they tried their hands at the new game of canasta.

But the real thrill for Katherine was when she saw the way in which Judy had greeted her stepfather when she first arrived. Not with averted gaze and tight lips like the old Judy, forcing herself to be polite, but with real friendliness.

"How's our Robert?" she had asked.

And Robert had grinned and answered in a broad Lancashire dialect:

"Eh, lass, fine; and how's our Judy?"

Just those few silly words, but the mother's heart thrilled with relief. For it seemed obvious that her two darlings had buried the hatchet, and what more could she ask of life?

Then the new maid had arrived from Denmark, and proved a very excellent, hard-working girl and an attractive personality to have about the place—to say nothing of being a good cook. So Katherine was able to abandon the pots and pans and go back to her typewriter, which was something of a relief, although Robert, wrinkling his nose over some of the strange Scandinavian dishes placed before him, continued to declare that his Kath was the better cook of the two.

However, Wilma had settled down nicely and was fast learning some English, and, because of her rosy cheeks, blue eyes and corn-coloured braids of hair, was already a great favourite with all the farm workers, who affectionately nicknamed her "Willy." She had also become a favourite with the dogs, which was a relief to Katherine, who felt that she could now get away for a day or two if she wished, and safely leave her pets with the animal-loving Wilma, who was, herself, born and bred on a Danish farm.

Cooltye Farm was prospering. Robert seemed the happiest of men, and Katherine's own marriage was an unqualified success. The only fly in the ointment at the moment was the fact that Pat was in Malaya. Katherine hated her son to be so far from her, in that unrestful country, but she looked forward to his home-coming in a year or two's time, and, as she often told herself, she was a very lucky woman in so many ways that she would be wicked to complain.

"What are you looking so serious about, Mum?" asked Judy as she put on her coat and scarf.

"Just thinking," said Katherine, "how much I love my whole family and wish I could have you all with me here for ever and ever."

They smiled into each other's eyes. Judy said:

"I think I can understand that. I wouldn't mind if Tony could get a job near by and we could all live together at the Farm. You can take it from me, I shan't really want to leave you and go back to town on Monday, except that it means being with my Tony."

"Then you really have been happy down here with us?"

"It's been absolutely *super*," said Judy warmly, "and you've been an angel to me. I haven't eaten so much for ages, and I've slept like a top."

"Well, you're looking all the better for it, darling."

"And now we've only got to wait for Tony's news," said Judy.

Yes, that was what they were waiting for now. The result of Tony's final examinations. It wasn't until Judy got down here that she realized how right Robert had been and how selfish it would have been of her to stay up in London and make any sort of demands upon her husband while he was sitting for those all-important Finals. When he had come down to Cooltye last Saturday he had looked tired out, although he had assured her it was mostly his cold that was pulling him down, and not excessive work. But it was obvious that he was being well fed and taken care of by his doting parents, and that being with them had made things materially more comfortable for him than if he had been up in the flat with a wife who was not well enough to "do the stairs."

Judy felt that she would always be grateful to Robert for having taken the trouble to argue some sense into her in the hospital that day. But she *was* longing to be with Tony again. She had missed him dreadfully, and in spite of all the luxury down here she had a sneaking longing for the little one-roomed flat which was their home.

They couldn't see the future very clearly at the moment. Everything depended on what sort of a job Tony could find for a start *if* he qualified.

"Oh, lord, Mummy! What on earth would happen if Tony didn't get through!" Judy suddenly burst out, as these thoughts raced through her head.

Katherine stood up and patted her shoulder.

"He will, darling. Robert and I both feel quite sure about that."

"I feel sure, too, really," said Judy with a laugh.

"Well, stop worrying and go along down to the stores for me, darling. Wilma will give you the list, and we want another box of *glacé* cherries. I'm going to show Wilma how I make a cherry cake."

Judy smacked her lips.

"Mum's cherry cake . . . nothing Wilma could do could possibly be better!"

"Take the dogs," added Katherine.

Judy, with furrowed brows, said:

"I wonder what time we shall get the news from Tony?"

"Wasn't he to ring you as soon as he saw the list?"

"Yes, he said so. And then he's coming straight down here. . . ."

Mother and daughter looked out of the window. It was one of those brisk March days with little white clouds scudding across a pale-blue sky. It was windy but not cold, and there was a crispness in the air. In Katherine's garden there were masses of yellow daffodils and borders of exquisitely blue scilla. No more snow or ice, nor stark, brown trees, but fresh green buds and the promise of spring. In the distance the Downs looked clear and beautiful, dappled by passing shadows. It was the sort of day on which Cooltye Farm was at its best. Everything, thought Katherine, held such promise. New life stirring; new hope. Even the pair of ducks on the pond out there were swimming around, proudly followed by a brood of small, downy, quacking children. They were getting more eggs on the chicken farm. There was a new calf. Robert was talking of buying a more modern kind of tractor, and engaging another farm-hand.

She could see him down there, talking to one of the lads.

He looked fit and youthful despite his thinning hair. Her heart swelled with pride and with thankfulness for the destiny which had led her to join forces with him. She loved him very much. She had loved him for a long time, and it was only the thought of the children which had held her back from marriage. The break with Judy had been a sharp grief, but even that had passed now. All was right with her world.

She turned from the window and followed Judy out of the room. This was no time to grow sentimental. She was in the middle of a children's book and she must get to work. She wanted to make some money so that there was something in hand for young Pat when he came out of the Army. She would write to him tomorrow. She would be able to tell him about Tony. It would be rather fun having a real live doctor for a son-in-law, she thought happily.

There was no telephone call from Tony that morning, nor even after lunch. Katherine and Robert both smiled at Judy's anxious face.

"It'll be all right . . . you'll hear in good time," Robert said consolingly.

"I'm sure he's failed!" said Judy tragically.

Katherine laughed.

"I'm sure you're not sure of anything of the kind."

"No, he couldn't," added Judy under her breath. "He's much too clever."

"Don't think about it," said her mother.

"Wouldn't you, if it was Robert?"

Katherine exchanged glances with her husband and then laughed again.

"Certainly, I'd be in a dither."

The telephone bell rang. Judy tore out to the hall. She returned with a disappointed face.

"That was the Vicar, reminding us that we all promised to go to tea there on Sunday. It's their anniversary or something."

"They're dear old things. We must go," said Katherine. Judy set her teeth.

"Oh, I wish I could learn to be patient. I'd give my soul

to know what Tony is doing at this very moment. I feel like rushing up to London."

"Take the car, if you want it," said Robert generously.

"Oh, but Rob, darling," Katherine said quietly, "you know we've got to go into Brighton. In fact we ought to be starting now. Don't you remember your appointment about the hen food?"

Robert had forgotten. He sprang up and rushed upstairs to change out of his corduroy breeches and boots. Twenty minutes later Judy was alone. Her mother and stepfather had driven off. She sat in front of the fire with the dogs at her feet, smoking, trying to possess her soul in patience.

By half past three she felt desperate and was driven to telephone through to her "in-laws." There was no reply to this call. Gloomily she put the receiver down and then 'phoned through to *Fleurette*. All she got out of that was a nice chat with Elizabeth, who didn't happen to be busy in the shop, but who said she would be thankful to see Judy back next week. The temporary girl who was helping her *looked* decorative, but didn't know how to handle flowers, she said. But of Tony she had no news.

"I expect everything's all right and you'll hear soon," she said, and rang off.

Four o'clock. Still no call from Tony. Judy was now in a ferment. She began to believe that he really *had* failed and was afraid to ring and tell her so. She smoked far too many cigarettes, walked up and down the room, fell over Pip and Squeak several times, and wondered if Tony were still alive. Perhaps he had drowned himself, she reflected, and giggled at this impossible idea. Then she began to feel genuinely anxious again. Surely something had happened. He should have had the big news by this time, and oh, why hadn't he rung?

She went to the front door and opened it. The sun had just gone in. It was blowing rather cold. These March days were short. Mummy and Robert would be back from Brighton soon. Judy really began to feel quite miserable, and never in her life before had she wanted Tony so much. She had been away from him far too long, she decided. She would never leave him again, no matter how ill she was or what the situation happened to be.

189

She shivered as a gust of wind struck her. She was only wearing a light jersey and her slacks. Then, suddenly, just as she was about to close the door, she saw a familiar figure, hatless, coatless, with a long woollen scarf wound round his neck, striding down the drive, just passing the duckpound.

With a scream of excitement Judy dashed out into the chilly dusk. She no longer felt the cold. Her whole body burned with excitement. For it was Tony himself. He hadn't 'phoned. He had *come* in person to tell her the news.

She reached him and he opened his arms wide and locked her in a bear hug.

"Darling. . . . Ju-Ju . . . my poppet!" he said.

"Oh, *Tony*!"

She held him close to her and lifted her eager mouth for his kisses.

"Tony, tell me. Why didn't you ring? What's happened?"

"I didn't ring because I felt I wanted to see you," he said. "And I only just had time to catch the train, so I dashed into it."

She sighed ecstatically, rubbed her glowing cheek against his, then looked at him with fond, anxious gaze.

"Oh, you do look so tired. You need a long rest like I've had, and the good air down here."

"Well," said Tony, "if that very nice mother of yours would like to put up with me, I might snatch a week at Cooltye."

"Down here, with *me*?"

"But of course."

"Then you're a free man? You've . . . you've got through?" she stammered, and caught her breath with excitement.

Tony released her, stepped back a pace and bowed from the waist.

"Madam, Dr. Anthony Chapman, at your service. Have you a liver? Are there spots before your eyes? Is your heart palpitating . . .?"

"Tony!" she interrupted with a cry, and her eyes looked like stars. "Oh, Tony, you *have* qualified!"

He nodded, and his handsome eyes glowed back into hers. "Rather fun, isn't it? It's the end and it's the beginning, my sweet, the real beginning of the story of Dr. and Mrs. Tony Chapman."

"Oh, Tony," she repeated rapturously, "how simply *super!*"

He caught her in his arms again.

"Mrs. Chapman's heart *is* palpitating a trifle on the fast side," he whispered.

"Can you wonder?" she giggled.

"Let's go in and have a cup of tea," he said, laughing, "and what's the betting my mamma-in-law has made a cherry cake?"

"She has. She made it this morning especially for you."

Tony gave a long sigh, picked up the small suitcase which he had dropped and, putting an arm round his wife's slender shoulder, walked with her into the warm welcoming atmosphere of Coolyte Farm, followed by the leaping, barking dogs.

IN HOLLYWOOD, WHERE DREAMS DIE QUICKLY, ONE LOVE LASTS FOREVER . . .

"I love you," she said. "I've loved you since the sun first rose. . . . My love has no shame, no pride. It is only what it is, always has been and always will be."

The words are spoken by Brooke Ashley, a beautiful forties film star, in the last movie she ever made. She died in a tragic fire in 1947.

A young screenwriter in a theater in Los Angeles today hears those words, sees her face, and is moved to tears. Later he discovers that he wrote those words, long ago; that he has been born again—as she has.

What will she look like? Who could she be? He begins to look for her in every woman he sees . . .

A Romantic Thriller
by
TREVOR MELDAL-JOHNSEN

AVON

41897
$2.50